The ABACUS Protocol

Thea Gregory

www.PlanetThea.com

ISBN (book) 978-0-9877347-7-8
ISBN (ebook) 978-0-9877347-8-5

One

The boom of the rocket's engines filled the air, and Vivian Skye's lungs. Her eyes went wide and her hand covered her mouth as the spacecraft took flight, climbing into the Auroran sky. Tendrils of red and green fire twisted together, dancing with the flow of the planet's magnetic fields. The rocket passed through one curtain of color, and then another, its trail threading through the few patches of blue present in the late morning sky. She squinted as the spacecraft climbed towards Helios, the Auroran sun. Using a finger to blot out the yellow might of the star, she watched the ascent until her eyes were squeezed shut.

This was her first visit to the spaceport in the capital city of Antica, Aurora's only major link to the stars. Vivian swallowed and gripped the rail. Her eyes traced, and retraced the smoke parting the dancing green and red lights. She chewed the inside of her lip, her mind working to understand why the totality of leaving Aurora was so difficult to process.

Somebody snickered behind her, and she turned to face the noise.

"They weren't kidding when they said Aurorans were hicks." The speaker was a tall man with beady eyes and a sagging chin. His skin was too pale to be from Aurora, and he sneered at Vivian as their eyes connected.

"Yeah, it's just a rocket. Those have been around for almost a thousand years," said an equally pale woman. Vivian's arms crossed and she pretended to read a street sign as she backed against the rail.

"Just don't eat the vegetables and you won't turn blue like them, okay honey?" the man said as they turned away. Vivian hung her head as her face flushed, the glory of the rocket launch all but forgotten. At the university, offworlders had been kind and respectful—she hadn't expected such unkind remarks on her own planet. It had taken almost two hundred years after colonization for the Auroran people to begin to evolve and adapt to their harsh world; a few vegetables would make no difference to an individual. Her mouth opened, but words escaped her.

The pair looked behind them and walked away, their gaze set in front of them. Vivian ran her fingers through her hair as she watched them leave.

"Ignore those idiots. They're just sore because I cleaned them out at poker." A deep but cheerful voice appeared next to her, loud enough that the couple turned back to glare at him before scurrying off.

Vivian turned and pursed her lips before responding. "I guess they ignored the tourist guide," she said, smirking. The man smiled, his bright white teeth contrasting against his reddish-blue lips. His cropped hair held a slight hint of blue pigmentation in the sunlight, known as blueberry blonde on Aurora.

"The paragraph that recommends avoiding 'friendly' games with the locals is gold, and they never listen. Ego.

Such a liability." He smiled as his eyes scanned her face, and continued: "Are you heading off-world?"

"Yes, I'm on the thirteen hundred express shuttle," she replied, leaning back against the rails overlooking the city. She'd arrived early to watch the ships take off, to try to ease her anxiety about spaceflight. It hadn't helped—the knot in her stomach grew with every ignition.

"I knew it," he said, pointing to the ground at her feet. "I stood right where you are for three hours my first time. You never see them taking off from back home, on the Borealis Plains. My name's Sven, by the way." He smiled as he watched the dissipating trail of smoke in the sky. The rumbling persisted, forcing Vivian to lean closer to Sven to make out his name.

"Well, hi Sven! Oh, wow, you've really been off world? How many times? And, I'm Vivian, from Australis Valley," she said. She had seldom spoken to anybody who had left Aurora. The professors from other planets and visiting dignitaries simply didn't understand the mystery and intrigue that Aurorans associated with space travel. Her cheeks grew hot, and she turned away from him to look at the city.

"This will be my fifth time. I don't think it will ever get boring. Where are you off to, southerner?" the man said, leaning against the metal bars and looking down at Antica's low skyline. Red brick buildings sprawled to the horizon, seldom exceeding three stories in height.

"I don't know if you've heard of it, but I got an internship working on the Extra-Galactic Observatory," Vivian said, hoping he wasn't a luddite. After the ABACUS incident, Aurora had received an influx of immigrants seeking refuge from the perceived threat of sentient artificial intelligence.

"I haven't heard of it. What's the closest planet?"

"New Damascus is where I catch a shuttle," she said. While the trip through the wormhole singularity would be nearly instantaneous, the Extra-Galactic Observatory was an unglamorous four weeks by shuttle from New Damascus, in stasis.

"That's at the edge of the galactic arm! Why under the lights would you want to go all the way out there?" he said, taking a step back. She could understand his reaction; there were many other observatories, even one just outside the Helios star system.

"I wanted to work with their computer, quIRK. It's a unique opportunity, because there are so few deep-space quantum computers that are as advanced and new as it is." She spoke the words too fast, one tumbling out after another.

"quIRK?" repeated Sven as he raised an eyebrow. "Sounds like some kind of particle. What's that stand for?"

"Well, the 'q' and the 'u' are for quantum, and IRK is an inside joke about how irritating the system was to design. Physicists and computer scientists have been historically notorious for picking humorous names," she said. She smiled, relieved that he wasn't overreacting; there really was nothing to be afraid of. quIRK was just a machine, only similar to ABACUS in design fundamentals.

"You know, I got to talk to one of the quantum computers with a basic personality and a human speech interface on Nova Albion. It's scary how smart it was. Think you can teach this quIRK to play poker?" he said, laughing.

"I'd love to try. quIRK is supposed to have pretty good social skills, I'd like to see him try to bluff."

"So, it's a *him*, now?" Sven crinkled his brow.

Vivian sucked in a quick breath. "It just doesn't seem right to refer to him as *it*, when he has a male voice, so why not?"

"Fair enough," he said with a shrug. "How about we go clear out some more offworlders before our shuttle leaves? I'll be with you at least until the central hub at Epsilon Eridani." His eyes twinkled and his grin returned.

"Can you see Sol from there?" Vivian had always wanted to see Earth, but that had been made impossible after humanity had destroyed the only singularity conduit to the system in response to the emerging ABACUS intelligence.

"It's small, but there are signs pointing to it. I'll show you when we get there. The shipyards in the asteroid belt are also a sight to behold."

"I can't wait! Okay, let's go find some easy marks. I want to have some fun before I go," Vivian said as she flashed Sven a wolfish smile. She was relieved to not have to spend the trip lost and alone.

Two

Vivian was strapped into her seat, deep within the confines of the rocket. The Spartan metal interior was a stark contrast from the natural earth-tones and blues of Auroran decor. The chair pressed into her spine, its padding insufficient for the high gravity environment. Sven had arranged to be moved to the seat next to her. She was sitting by the window—all she could see was the infinite ripple of the lights. Anything more than a quick glance sent her vision spinning and her stomach threatening to empty itself of every meal she'd ever eaten. She and Sven hadn't managed to find a poker victim, but they had instead idled away the hour talking about Sven's exports. He was trying to establish a luxury

11

business selling Auroran flutes to offworld music programs, with great success. Vivian played the Auroran flute herself, although she didn't consider herself to be more than an enthusiastic amateur. She hoped it would be a good way to make friends, if the flutes were as popular as Sven indicated.

"Relax, it will be okay. It's really fun, and haven't you always wondered what the moons look like without the lights dancing over them?" Sven whispered in her ear.

She smiled, and realized that her knuckles had turned white from her grip on the restraints and her jaw had clenched itself shut. "I'll try," Vivian said. She scanned the other passengers. Some were sleeping. How could anyone sleep at a time like this? They were sitting on a giant bomb!

"Don't look at them; you'll miss what's going on outside the window. Out there is way more interesting. I bet you can't tell the moons apart!" Sven was teasing her, now.

"Oh come on, I can tell the moons apart." Vivian said, chuckling, fixing her eyes on the chairs in the aisle across from them.

"Okay, what's the true color of Aeos?" he asked, running a hand through his hair. It stood up in a shock of blueberry spikes.

"Aeos is the only moon that's actually white. Pyrois, Aethon and Phlegon are all captured asteroids and grey." She felt silly at being able to recite the grade school lesson from memory, almost twenty years later. At least she could still pronounce the tongue-twisting names. Why couldn't they name planets and moons after something other than ancient Terran mythological figures?

"Somebody remembers primary school!" Sven said, clasping his hands in front of him and talking through pursed lips. "Good to know living inside a mountain for five years didn't blind you to the natural radiance of our world."

"It's only a fifteen minute elevator ride to the surface, you know," Vivian said, rolling her eyes. "Some of us cave dwellers like fresh air." The temptations of readily available electronic entertainment, movies and interactive games often blinded young Aurorans to the low-tech surface world. Even the silent and inhuman quantum computer at the university was an interesting novelty.

"Just checking." Sven was cut off by a recorded voice instructing them to stay seated and to not remove the restraints. Vivian wasn't going to let go until they were safely in orbit and en route to the transport singularity. She clamped her jaw shut, determined not to scream as soon as the ignition sequence started.

The ship lurched, and Vivian swallowed hard and fought not to hold her breath. Her heartbeat rattled against her ribs. She stared at the plain steel ceiling of the ship and willed herself to be calm. Much of this rocket-based technology was over one thousand years old, she reminded herself. Advanced anti-gravity systems would not function in the Helios system, and the space propulsion system was unsafe to use within a planet's atmosphere. Thus, re-usable chemical rockets had made a comeback.

Vivian pressed against her chair. Her chest grew heavy, but the discomfort was manageable. A quick check outside the window showed Aurora's pale blue sky spattered with dancing green and red lights. Sven grinned at her, stretching his arms behind his head and feigning yawning. His errant bravado soothed her nerves. Some of the sleeping passengers awakened. Suddenly, the sky went black, and Vivian could see the stars unobstructed for the first time in her life. She couldn't believe how many of them there were! Usually, she could see the brightest local stars, such as Vega and Sirius along with Aurora's four moons, and maybe Betelgeuse on a rare night when Helios' intense storms quieted. She'd seen pictures of space, but it was nothing like actually being there. She craned her neck, wanting to take in everything. There was so much to see!

"Looking for something?" Sven asked.

"I was hoping to see Aeos." Vivian blushed, not wanting to embarrass herself by claiming to be spellbound by the stars.

"Not this time, I'm afraid. Sit back and enjoy the trip," he said as he closed his eyes.

A metallic voice announced that their travel time to the Aurora Singularity Connection was eight hours, and that gravity had been set to Earth Standard. Vivian had never felt so light before—her limbs moved too quickly, and her heart seemed to float in her chest. She looked out the window, and watched with both elation and despair as Aurora, the only home she'd ever known, shrank into the distance. She saw a white flash just over the northern continent, and hoped it was Aeos.

The restraints popped free, and she twisted around for a better look. Aurora had become a pale blue dot, but she hoped to spot some of the other planets, especially the gas giant, Hyperion. Like Aurora, it had brilliant persistent lights that were a spectacular sight from space. Vivian hopped out of her seat, and her arm flew back and whacked Sven in the face.

"Hey! Watch where you swing those!" Sven rubbed his nose, which had reddened.

"I'm so sorry!" she said, feeling her face flush.

"You're fifty percent stronger now. Take a walk and get used to it before we get to the hub." He returned to slouching in his chair, and tested his nose with his fingers.

She stood up, taking great care to keep track of all her limbs. They were not long, as she was just about average height, but she had a powerful build and now understood that she didn't know her own strength in standard Earth gravity. Cramming her hands into her pockets, she shuffled towards the window to stargaze.

Three

The trip through the singularity wormhole had been exhilarating, but brief. As they approached the large, steel-enclosed ring, Vivian could only see a starless void ahead of them. She wasn't used to total, complete night. On Aurora, the skies were perpetually lit, and there had been artificial lights everywhere in the subterranean university. It had never occurred to Vivian that anyone could seriously be afraid of the dark, but as she stared into that artificial singularity, the walls seemed to close in, drawing that black point into an infinite maw. Her breath caught in her throat—she had to will herself to keep breathing. So many possibilities flooded into her mind—the controlled singularity could lose containment and smash them into subatomic particles, or one wrong calculation could result in a premature ejection from the wormhole, marooning them in the emptiness of uninhabited space. It had taken decades, and sometimes even centuries, for stasis ships to establish new hubs for rapid travel and colonization, and the Aurora colony predated the network altogether. Her heart raced, and she gasped for breath.

A hand clasped around her shoulder, shaking her. She spun to face it. Sven cocked his head and peered at her. "Are you okay?" he asked.

Vivian blinked a few times. She opened her mouth, but words escaped her.

"It's all right, Vivian." He squeezed her shoulder. "This is the safest way to travel. There haven't been any accidents on the network in centuries."

Vivian forced out a slow breath and nodded.

He smiled. "It will be fine. Trust me. If it's not fine, I'll send you a new flute free of charge."

Vivian chuckled and found her voice. "How will you send me a flute if we're lost in space?"

He frowned. "Don't think too hard about that one. It might rip space-time. Now, enjoy the show."

There was no sensation of movement or bright flash of light when they entered the aperture, as opposed to their violent take-off. The stars re-emerged, and ahead of her lay an imposing space station. It was an immense rectangular metallic structure, with indents where hundreds of tiny ships were nestled. Red and green lights flashed along the alcoves, and windows ran outside the periphery of the intermediate levels. Vivian had never seen anything so impossible, or so huge. Even at a distance, it dwarfed the ring of hubs that honeycombed around it. With nothing of similar size to put the giant prism in perspective, it seemed large enough to be its own planet.

"You know how I know it's your first time in space?" Sven's voice was dry, but his smile remained warm.

"Oh, sorry," Vivian said, without taking her eyes off the monstrosity in front of them. She couldn't believe something so large could have been built in space.

"You'll get used to it. How long until your connection?" Sven maintained his easy-going disinterest in the structure. She noticed that he avoided looking at it.

"I have about two hours to figure out how to get there," she said, frowning as she acknowledged that she had no idea of how to find the ship to New Damascus.

"Fortunately, what they don't tell you is that over half of that *thing* is empty and sealed. They're still waiting for teams to reach all those new systems to establish a hub." Sven laughed as he spoke.

"What's so funny about that?" she asked, hoping that he wasn't laughing at her.

"Humanity isn't known for its long-term planning capabilities. The fact that they've planned for hubs that won't be open for hundreds of years is kind of funny."

"I see your point. You have to wonder about the people who voluntarily go into stasis for hundreds of years, though." She contemplated her own imminent four week stasis trip, something she tried very hard not to think about.

"You know, they're probably very well rested," he said, stretching.

Vivian doubted that even stasis could make her relax. She hadn't managed to sleep on the shuttle at all, and she had only nibbled on the complimentary meal.

They disembarked the ship in silence, and she stepped onto the Epsilon Eridani station. She was surprised by how spacious it was on the inside, the ceiling stretching up almost twenty meters. The large metallic chamber was bisected by a conveyor belt for rapid passenger movement. A collection of shops and depots lined the far wall, and an eclectic assortment of humanity wandered the giant corridor. Smells of greasy food wafted about the room, mixing with the stale air. People bumped into her, and she pushed back, trying to stay with her guide.

"Okay, I have to leave you here," Sven said. "I need to get my cargo out of storage on Phaeton, and that's going to take longer than you have. Check a terminal for your directions." He paused, and handed her a small yellow plastic wafer. He continued: "Here's my Gal-Net contact, when you get yours set up drop me a line. You never know when you can use a friend out here."

"Oh, thanks. I will. You've been too great, thank you," she said, securing the small card in the pocket of her cotton pants.

"If some egghead gets fresh with you, just punch him. Trust me—they won't know what hit them. And keep exercising, or going back home will not be fun," he said with a wink.

"I can take care of myself. Just make sure you don't humiliate the wrong poker player."

"I'll take my chances." He darted in, and planted a quick kiss on her cheek before departing. She stumbled for a moment, hoping her awkwardness would go unnoticed. She then walked off, glancing back to see Sven vanish into the crowd. Her hand shot to her cheek, stroking the afterimage of his lips. Had she spent so much time in a mountain, surrounded by machines and the people equally enamored of them that she could no longer pick up on basic social cues?

The thought followed her to the terminal—Janus, the station's AI was online and ready to assist her. She'd worked with some similar units at university, and after two attempts she was able to discover the route to the

New Damascus port. She counted herself fortunate that the directions didn't involve the rapid conveyor belts. Her instincts interpreted them as unsafe.

She walked towards her destination with a canvas bag flung over her shoulder and her luggage already on its way. The station was designed with a wing for every arm of the Milky Way galaxy. New Damascus was located near a gap in the galaxy's Cygnus arm, and its port was in a newer part of the station. After a few minutes, she spotted the bend in the hallway and marched towards it.

A stark contrast in decor was evident as she walked through the threshold of the corridor. Gone was the polished steel and granite motif, replaced by authentic-looking ceramic tiles and warm wood tones. It was as though she'd stepped off the space station and into a cozy traditional home. The wing itself was about the size of a soccer field, and was cordoned off at the end by a large steel barrier. There were only two ports: one to the New Damascus orbital spaceport, and the other restricted to the Ithaca Colonization Initiative. The door slid open as she passed her ticket over the scanner. She took a seat by the window, and fell asleep as she awaited departure.

Four

Vivian awoke with a start, and pressed her hands against the hatch of the stasis tube in a futile attempt to force it open. Her fingers found only cold steel and no give. She was confused and groggy as the events from the hours before her entry into stasis resurfaced in her mind. She'd been asleep for four weeks, but it was as though she'd just closed her eyes moments ago. The five meter long pod she'd taken to the Extra-Galactic Observatory was un-manned; it would be up to the station's complement of researchers to help her disembark. The staff at the New Damascus space dock had loaded her bags into the pod, and secured her in stasis before the craft embarked on its lonely voyage. It had already been filled to capacity with care packages from the crew's families and new equipment. After seeing the cramped and disordered conditions, Vivian had welcomed traveling in stasis.

Voices murmured outside her tube, but the window above her remained dark. Banging vibrated through the tube as boxes and equipment were moved around. She hoped they were being careful; those boxes held important fragile parts for the upgrade she was going to perform on quIRK. Her work could be delayed by even the slightest scratch. The air inside the tube was growing hot and stale; its life support system had been deactivated as soon as the Extra-Galactic Observatory's computer had cleared the docking procedure. quIRK knew she was here. Why hadn't he told the staff?

Her cheeks blossomed pink, and she hammered her fists against the tube's canister, the stagnant air leaving her dizzy and her sight blooming with bright red spots. How could they leave her like this for so long? The voice spoke again, and she heard the clatter of items being moved. She couldn't make out the words, but one of the voices reverberated through the canister—it was soft, but steady and commanding. The other presence had gone quiet and occupied itself with clearing the fallen debris from on top of her pod. She reasoned that her small craft must have encountered some kind of turbulence in the interplanetary medium. She wanted to keep calm, but her heart was pounding against her burning lungs. Why was only one of them working to free her?

The lid cracked open, treating Vivian to a welcome wave of cool air which soothed her burning lungs. Inhaling, she squinted at the streak of harsh white light.

"Hey, are you okay?" She couldn't see the speaker; he had a deep but concerned voice.

"Groggy, kind of." Her voice worked to overcome her dry throat. She opened her eyes to a pair of brown eyes peeking out from under a nest of overgrown wavy, black hair.

"I told you there was a passenger, Alec." The other voice spoke. Its tone was so perfect and even, a gentle tenor. It was a voice that resounded like a calm wave across the ocean.

"Yeah, well," Alec said as he threw open the lid. "Last time you said that it was just that damn pair of kittens you'd ordered." He extended a hand to Vivian. She found the conversation very odd. She could only just make out his features; he had a thin face with fine features and round, thick lips. His complexion was reddish—unlike anything she'd encountered in Aurora. She tried not to stare.

"Allow me to introduce Vivian Skye—" the speaker continued, before it was cut off by Alec.

"She's blue! We need oxygen down here!" The young man grasped her wrist, groping for a pulse. His wide eyes searched her face. Vivian checked her arms and hands in alarm, awareness rushing back to her. She didn't seem any bluer than usual.

"No need for alarm, Alec," said the other voice. "She's an Auroran, and perfectly healthy." The voice hadn't altered, in tone or pitch. How could he know she was healthy if he couldn't see her?

"Wow, okay, that was unexpected. Sorry Vivian, let me get you out of that tube." He sucked in a deep breath before pulling her to her feet with a grimace of his pouting lips. She stepped out. Her legs ached from lack of use, but the strain wasn't unpleasant. She peered out behind Alec.

"Um, hi Alec. Who's your friend?"

"*Friend*, yeah, that's an interesting word for him," Alec said with an exaggerated shake of his head, before drawing his face close to hers and taking a good look at her skin. She pulled back, fighting the need to cover her heating cheeks.

"Are you insinuating something, Alec?" Despite the insult, there was no anger in the voice, or any hint of emotion at all.

"Damn, he usually doesn't catch sarcasm." Alec rolled his eyes. "That's just quIRK. You'll get used to him eventually."

"That's quIRK?" Vivian couldn't contain her surprise. She searched the ceiling, the walls, even the ridged metal floor. She didn't see any cameras, flashing lights, terminals or speakers. There was nothing to indicate that any kind of computer was in the room, much less one of the most advanced artificial intelligences in the galaxy. It was so unlike how things had been at school. Alec began to laugh.

"Mind your manners, Alec. We want Vivian to feel welcome. After all, she is performing my upgrades." quIRK's voice had dropped, as though it were trying to whisper.

A discreet computer, how interesting, Vivian thought. "You know about that?" Vivian asked, as Alec made no effort to compose himself.

"Of course. I do have a vested interest in making sure you do a good job."

Vivian caught herself nodding—she couldn't believe she was empathizing with a computer. But, it was a machine which had been programmed to be a companion and social outlet for crews on isolated deep-space missions. Still, she hadn't expected him to seem so alive. Maybe not human or even self-aware, but perhaps he was simultaneously more and less than human.

"I'll do my best." She was not quite sure how to respond to that statement.

"I expect nothing less." quIRK returned his voice to full volume, and continued: "Now, Alec, you drew the antiblue quark in the probability pool, so it's your job to finish unloading the shuttle."

"I drew the antiblue quark the last two cycles too. I think you're cheating. Shouldn't I help Vivian get to her room?" Alec spoke to the wall as his gaze followed the chaotic mess of spilled boxes surrounding him.

"I am perfectly capable of showing Miss Skye to her quarters. Probability is a bitch, Alec." Once again, quIRK pitched his voice to a whisper.

Vivian couldn't help but laugh.

"You laugh now; wait until he decides he wants you to draw antiblue. What the hell is antiblue anyways?" Alec asked, grumbling as he checked the label on a box.

"It's my favorite color," quIRK said. "Now, if you'll follow the red panels on the floor, Vivian, I'll show you your new home."

"How could I resist? See you later, Alec." Vivian bit back a rush of questions. Butterflies danced in her stomach. She was alone with quIRK! The computer at her university couldn't speak, much less antagonize humans with a favorite color. She told herself that it was just a sophisticated psychological subroutine. There was no way quIRK could be sentient and allowed to continue to exist. He'd have been reported years ago.

She walked out of the dark shuttle, and she was surprised to be met by warm, cream-colored walls and a beige-tiled floor. None of this was as she expected. From her own limited research back on Aurora, she'd expected a clinical and metallic decor to the egg-shaped station. The external pictures that had accompanied her Aurora-friendly information package showed an oblong monstrosity with two hemispherical indents on each side that were lined with hexagonal telescope inputs, its grey-alloy surface only marred by a bisecting streak of windows. As quIRK guided her way down the hall by illuminating tiles, she could still hear his calm, impassive voice in the distance, debating the merits of antiblue with Alec.

Five

Vivian didn't see another person during her short walk through the facility. The red tiles blinked ahead of her down the curved hallway, like in some of the old movies she'd watched. She tried to step on one, hoping that the color would change or flash, but instead the iridescent red vanished beneath her intruding foot. The fog of stasis was lifting from her mind, though her legs were still too light. She was glad to leave her bags behind with Alec, if only because she didn't want to accidentally break anything.

Something else bothered her, something that made the little hairs on the back of her neck stand up. It was quIRK. She'd anticipated a cold, obvious mechanical voice and a basic, utilitarian personality. That *thing* had a favorite color—although she doubted that antiblue could be described in the visual spectrum. Humans usually claimed puce as their preferred color when trying to annoy others. Perhaps antiblue could be interpreted as the quantum computer equivalent of puce? quIRK had not spoken, so she assumed that he was still arguing with Alec about quarks. She couldn't decide which of them was more ridiculous: quIRK for having a favorite color, or Alec for arguing with a computer about its favorite color.

"This is your room, Vivian," quIRK said as the tiles returned to their non-luminous state. The door slid open without a sound, and she stepped inside. "This station has one long elliptical hallway. While getting lost is theoretically impossible, some humans have managed to do so. Please ask me should you need further assistance."

"Thanks," she said, unsure of how to speak to it. Were manners even necessary? Also troubling was the concept of getting lost in a space station that had only one hallway.

"I have prepared these quarters for you. If you like, I can adjust the gravity and oxygen levels to be closer to the Auroran standard," quIRK continued. The door slid closed behind her, but she still couldn't discern where his voice was coming from. The effect was disconcerting, heightening the sense that quIRK was an all-seeing, omnipresent being.

"That would be great!" she said, relieved that even if she was a long way from home on a strange space station for the next year or more, she could at least be comfortable in her own room. The lightness in her limbs and chest subsided. She rolled her shoulders while she walked over to the window that spanned the length and height of her room. There were a few distant specs of light, but otherwise the interstellar vista was a dark and lonely void.

"You look more relaxed already. Alec will be along with your bags shortly. If you need anything, just call. I am everywhere," quIRK said. Vivian was a little unnerved by the concept of being watched by a computer, but at least he was a thoughtful computer.

Vivian rubbed down the stand of gooseflesh on her arms as she examined her small room; compared to the cramped and overcrowded dormitory room she'd shared with three other girls at the Auroran Technological Institute, it was luxurious. The bed was about double the size of her old cot, and, after a test-flop, she estimated that it was several decades newer. There was a simple metal dresser and mirror built into the wall by the foot of the bed. Across the room sat a computer terminal and a comfortable chair made of a shiny black material. Vivian ran a finger along it, trying to place the fabric. There was a small, private bathroom set in polished metal just behind the desk. She'd never had her own bathroom before—her home back on Aurora had been small and cramped, with her parents and two brothers. They had all shared a single bathroom, and she had been the only child with the privilege of having her own room.

She sighed when she thought about her family, and gazed out into the barren twilight of intergalactic space. Her parents had been ardent traditionalist luddites who believed that advanced technology was enslaving the human spirit. They also despised Caesareans, for reasons beyond Vivian's comprehension. For a long time, she'd tried to hide her passion for technology and quantum informatics from them. She'd passed her intense study off as wanting to become a botanist, to follow in her mother's footsteps. However, when the time came to finalize her specialization, she picked quantum informatics at the only school on Aurora that was equipped to teach it. Her mother had been heartbroken, prompting her father to issue an ultimatum: school or family. The choice still tormented her, but she knew she could never be happy or even fulfilled taking over her mother's bluespargus and rice farm, or being apprenticed to a trade. Her older brother, Gareth, had been more supportive—he had helped her move into the dorms and written her letters after she'd been kicked out of the house, but after a few months he'd stopped replying. After that final abandonment, she'd flung herself at her schoolwork and made friends who were more than happy to be her new family, many of whom had also experienced a similar falling out. The pressure of rebuilding her social network after leaving Aurora was daunting, but she'd already met Sven, and Alec seemed like a nice person, if he could get used to her being a bit blue. She wasn't sure how quIRK figured into the picture. An eccentric uncle seemed the most apt comparison she could make to the supercomputer's personality.

The door buzzed, shattering her daydream, and she turned from the window. She walked towards it and pushed the small button on the panel next to the door. It slid open, and Alec was standing in front of her with a too-big smile on his face and her bags in his hands. "Room service has arrived. Where do you want your bags?" he asked, presenting a mouth that held the illusion of having too many teeth.

"Just leave them by the bed, please." She stepped out of the way and motioned him in.

"all right," Alec said. But, as he crossed the threshold, he stumbled under the weight of the bags. "Oh shit!" he cried out, and he fell to his knees. The bags toppled to the floor, her effects clattering inside.

"Are you all right?" Vivian rushed to help Alec to his feet. It hadn't occurred to her to warn him about the gravity. It was so normal to her, and usually visitors to Aurora were well aware of the challenges inherent to visiting that planet.

"A little warning next time. Did quIRK put you up to that?" Alec tried to push himself to his feet, but needed a moment to gather his strength. He pulled away from her, forcing himself to an upright position. Sweat beaded on his forehead.

"No, no of course not," she said, taking a step back. A seed of doubt had been planted—did quIRK intentionally suggest the gravity change as a prank? As far as she knew, no computer was programmed with a sense of humor.

"Come now, Alec. Vivian can have her quarters any way she likes." The smooth, clear voice was unmoved by the spectacle.

"You like it like this? What the hell?" Alec protested as he shambled to the door.

Vivian stifled a laugh. "It's how my world is! quIRK offered to change it so I would be more comfortable!"

"quIRK. I knew he was in on this," Alec said, grumbling as he stepped out of the room.

"Is twenty-five percent extra gravity really that difficult of an adaptation for a human?" quIRK asked.

"I'm from Elyssia, damn it. Normal gravity took me weeks of strength training to get used to." Alec sighed. He ran his hand through his messy hair. The wavelets tumbled back into place.

"I had no idea, I'm sorry," Vivian said. She realized that everything in her room would weigh close to double what he was accustomed to.

"See quIRK, she's sorry. What about you?" Alec talked to the ceiling, shaking his fist.

"I cannot perceive how this situation could be interpreted as my fault. Perhaps you should exercise more."

Alec walked off down the hall without so much as a goodbye while he continued to berate quIRK. "You are evil, quIRK. I hope she does upgrade you, you no-good particle-brained—"

Vivian remained silent, and slipped back into her room. The door closed behind her. She hefted her bags off the floor and carried them to the bed. Despite her disastrous reception so far, it was time to unpack, and to make sure her more fragile personal effects were not damaged during the trip to the station, or when Alec dropped them.

She sighed as she began putting her clothes into the dresser. Everything needed to be arranged properly. Shirts needed to be sorted by sleeve length and color, and they could not be in the same drawer as pants or undergarments. Those were some of the rules she'd imposed to keep her surroundings organized. Order was important to her, and her innate desire for neatness and reliability was a strong motivation in specializing in quantum informatics. She knew that critical thinking could solve any problem and assist her in conquering any hint of chaos in her life.

She shifted to the other bag, the one containing her favorite books and flute. Her room wasn't equipped with a bookshelf, but she could figure out an acceptable alternative for her choice selection of Auroran books. She found the open case of her flute and pulled it free, and then she found the crushed remains of her flute underneath it. "Oh no, no," she sighed as she examined it. It was as though she's been punched in the gut—her legs were weak and her breath caught in her lungs.

"What is wrong, Vivian?" quIRK asked.

"My flute got broken. I don't know if I can replace it," she said, tears trickling down her cheeks. It had been a gift from her mother, for Vivian's seventh birthday. She had little else to remember the woman by. Her warm smiles and their long talks were now a thing of the distant past. Because her father hadn't allowed her to retrieve her things after kicking her out of the family home, the flute was all she had left of her mother.

"I am sorry, Vivian. Would you like me to help you look for a replacement?"

"Do we get Gal-Net access? I might be able to order one from an exporter I met on the trip here," she said, remembering Sven's card in her back pocket. It wouldn't bring her old flute back, but she could still play. That was something positive, at least. Perhaps the music, rather than the flute, was the true gift.

"We have limited access. Because of time delays related to distance and bandwidth limitations, real-time access is impossible. Messages will take four days and five hours to reach New Damascus, and downloads may take longer based on available system resources."

"Can we receive personal packages here?"

"Yes, the shuttle docks twice per quarter. I will provide you with transit instructions," quIRK said, and the lights on her desk terminal lit up. He continued: "I have set up a Gal-Net account for you. Please complete the process and you will be able to access the common files and send messages."

"Good, I'll do that. Thank you." Vivian wiped the remaining tears from her eyes. They needed to be clear for the retinal scan, and she needed to get a grip. She set the broken flute on the bed, inside its case. It was made from a bamboo-like Auroran reed. They were fragile and very easy to snap or crush.

She sat down at the terminal, and submitted her retinal scan and handprint. Then, she managed to figure out how to use the adapted mail system and began typing a message to Sven. She would have dictated, but she didn't want quIRK commenting on every little thing, or for her feelings to seep through into the message. Vivian hoped he remembered her, and she was still cursing herself for being so awkward and clueless around him. She told him about the trip, and meeting quIRK for the first time. About how Alec had looked at her like she was an alien and his reaction to the gravity in her room. The experience was cathartic, but recounting how her precious flute had been crushed brought the tears back into her eyes. At the end, she asked if he could sell her an Auroran flute, and how much it would cost to have it shipped to the Extra-Galactic Observatory.

All she had left to do was to wait until morning, and her first meeting with her coworker and supervisor, Bryce Zimmer.

Six

Bryce Zimmer sighed as he shifted in his chair. The tingling in his lower back eased, but only for a moment. He clenched his toes and counted to three. He didn't want quIRK to register his discomfort. He was a middle-aged man of sixty years—he hadn't yet indulged in life-extending treatments, and today was one of the days his bones ached. His thick hands ran over the controls of his computer terminal, and he focused on preserving his dignity as he imagined a true Roman would. His office was adorned with the purple and gold tapestries and art of the Caesarean upper class.

Bryce blinked twice and took a deep breath. He was reviewing the plans for the upgrades that were to begin on quIRK. The work was straightforward—he could have it completed it in less than half the time allotted—but the New Damascus authorities had bought into the insipid idea of employing recent graduates, rather than favoring people of proven experience and breeding. He had better things to do than supervise some brat from a fancy technical school, like keeping quIRK in line. The latest reports indicated that quIRK now had a favorite color; this was even after the unspeakable kitten stunt! The ABACUS protocol—a set of instructions for preventing more machine awakenings—was a nightmare to properly enforce with quIRK; in many ways, that *machine* had skirted the grey areas bordering true sentience by design. More personally, and far more importantly, Bryce had his retirement to worry about. He needed to fire his investment manager back home on Caesarea, and retain the services of somebody who understood the need to be ruthless in life and economics. quIRK was speaking, but as usual, Bryce tuned him out so he could concentrate on the non-menial aspects of space station administration.

That *thing* was created to serve humans, not collaborate as an equal!

"You're not listening to me, Bryce," the machine said.

That perfect voice bored into his ears, but the mention of his name shook him from his thoughts. Twelve years of its incessant droning had created pinched lines next to his eyes and greyed his hair. It still presumed to speak with him as an equal!

"You were talking about preparations to rotate the station, I know." He spoke in a slow voice, as though he were speaking to a child—he didn't want to show his irritation. quIRK could be very invasive if it sensed weakness. Bryce knew he should not give quIRK the opportunity to dissect his psyche—not when it could record their conversation.

"The alpha-side telescopes require extensive repairs which can no longer be delayed," quIRK's voice continued droning on. His retirement had better be worth fifteen years of listening to quIRK.

"Fine, *fine*, come up with an equipment list and work schedule with Professor Schmidt and give it to me before the next requisitions deadline." He preferred to delegate the minutiae to quIRK. He had more important things to worry about than telescopes. When did galaxies make anyone rich?

"Very well. Should I tell Vivian to come see you, now?" quIRK asked.

"No, I think I'll just drop in on her later. Where is she?"

"She is working in the Informatics Diagnostic Lab, as assigned," quIRK replied.

"Good. Make sure she stays out of my hair."

"Should I tell her to avoid your sideburns, or the comb-over?"

Bryce's cheeks burned. "It was a figure of speech, damn it. Now leave me alone." He resolved to have a conversation with Alec about teaching quIRK sarcasm and humor. He ran his hand through his hair, messing it up. He was not desperate enough to attempt a comb-over —even if it would be years until he could indulge in the age-reversal drugs readily available on Caesarea. That monster was getting under his skin.

quIRK didn't speak again, though Bryce knew he was never truly alone. Most staff only occupied the station for one or two years before opting to leave or being offered a promotion. People tended to enjoy interacting with quIRK, though none of them knew the computer like Bryce did. For many, quIRK was a novelty, a fancy toy or an imaginary friend brought to life. They perceived him as harmless, and went about their lives. Similar to most technology, as long as it worked, they didn't need to care about it. However, Bryce knew the consequences of inaction and poor maintenance, or worse, somebody tampering with quIRK. Preventing another ABACUS incident was the real reason he'd been assigned to the station rather than wasting his talents on the consequences of hardware failures. That's what Alec was for. quIRK was fully capable of attending to all of the station's functions without him.

Bryce shifted in his chair, finding it was lumpy in the wrong places. He wanted to order a replacement, but he didn't want quIRK to know that his back was getting worse. Proof of ill-health could find him prematurely retired and forced to return to Caesarea in disgrace. He was so close to restoring his family's good name and undoing his father's mistakes.

He read through quIRK's operation logs, searching for references to kittens and colors. *What the hell is antiblue?* He wasn't certain he was looking at the right logs. quIRK was capable of misleading him, and had hidden vital information from him even prior to the kitten incident. Bryce had no proof quIRK was sentient; he simply could have mastered human social skills as he was programmed to do. Of course, Bryce hadn't executed the bi-yearly memory wipes, but those were only a formality and caused productivity delays while quIRK was forced to re-master previously acquired skills.

Securing adequate proof was a problem; nobody knew what construed proof. All records of ABACUS's awakening had been lost when the administrators at Epsilon Eridani had severed the hub link between Earth and the rest of the Milky Way. Bryce considered that to be a stupid, instinctive action that had deprived humanity of vital knowledge. How did ABACUS, Earth's primary computer, gain sentience? Perhaps it was an upgrade or experiment gone wrong, or it could be the natural and logical conclusion in the evolution of a sufficiently powerful artificial intelligence. Bryce knew that the latter had been deemed impossible by most experts, especially in post-ABACUS models like quIRK, but what if the experts were wrong? The ABACUS incident had happened more than a century ago, and quIRK was more advanced than ABACUS in every conceivable way. quIRK, however, had been designed with limits on how much processing power he could devote to an individual task—a handicap designed to prevent sentience. It didn't seem to stop quIRK from picking a favorite color, or deciding he liked cats, but Bryce observed that preferring cats wasn't an indicator of human intelligence either.

He looked up from the activity logs, helpless before the problem at hand. He was expected to enforce the ABACUS Protocol without any clear directions on how to diagnose a sentient artificial intelligence, or a realistic emergency plan for the event quIRK needed to be shut down. The Extra-Galactic Observatory was equipped with digital backup systems and interfaces for essential tasks, but they could not run the station with only a half-complement of five crewmembers and expect to complete their mission.

Bryce wondered if he could be imagining things—reading meaning into random events. Pets were shown to relieve stress; quIRK could have simply overheard somebody talking about their beloved childhood pet and unilaterally decided that a surprise pair of kittens would improve morale. Similarly, antiblue could be his attempt to fit in more with the human inhabitants—integration was important if he was going to monitor the crew for signs of stress, isolation, and space fever.

There was a possible solution—a new tool in his arsenal. Two months ago, he'd uncovered an interesting backdoor into quIRK's systems—a kind of programming loophole that could allow him to control and observe the stimulus fed into quIRK's awareness. He hadn't used it, yet, but it could be a useful avenue to investigate this anomalous behavior, or to converse with the machine with a modicum of privacy from the authorities.

Bryce sighed. He had better things to do, like monitor his Dynamo Quantronics stock, read financial reports, and tend to the business side of his family's vineyards back on Caesarea. He didn't care about the grapes; they could go straight to Hades as far as Bryce was concerned. However, his grandfather had loved the expanses of verdant life and left a stipulation in his will that it be maintained. It would make a pleasant enough estate, if he were inclined to repair the decaying cottage and relocate the slaves.

He stood up, and forced himself the bear the intense pain in his lower back with a smile. He may as well get the meeting the new girl over with—he hadn't bothered to read her file, but he was expecting an entitled little snot from Kanadia Prime. Kanadians had more implants than humanity, but at least they were good workers.

He was still far more concerned with his retirement's security than the damned alpha-telescope array.

Seven

Vivian was organizing her workspace, paying
meticulous attention to the mountain of parts that still
needed to be catalogued. The small lab had been a
disaster, filled with never-cleared debris left over from
the station's assembly. Spare parts littered the
workbenches, and opened boxes were stacked in the
center of the room. The access tunnels that lead to both
the station's computer core and reactors would be
inaccessible until she cleared the room. To make matters
worse, her own equipment was sitting in the hall. Before
she could verify that everything had survived the bumpy
trip, and Alec's unpacking skills, she needed to clear the
table. It seemed that even the room's environmental

controls had been neglected—a layer of dust had settled over everything, and her clothes and hair had been coated after a matter of minutes of digging around the room.

Vivian had made the mistake of attempting to dust off a box before handling it, resulting in a bout of violent sneezing. quIRK was working to find her some storage space for the extra equipment, and to arrange for Alec to fix the ventilation system. Vivian hoped that she would have the opportunity to clean both the lab and herself before her meeting with the administrator. Grime clung under her fingernails, and her clothes were smeared with lines of dust.

A cat yowled at her, and she jumped, almost dropping a box of assorted electronics. She spun to see a small tabby cat whose coat still had an element of kitten fuzziness standing in the open doorway. Vivian set the box down and walked over as it continued to plead for attention. She knelt down and stroked its soft fur, eventually picking the small beast up and cradling it in her arms. It was so small and delicate, and its green eyes looked into hers. Its needle-like claws prickled her chin.

"Aren't you sweet! What's your name?" she asked the kitten as she walked around the room.

"I see you've found my Lepton," quIRK said. The small cat gave no impression that it was aware of the disembodied voice. Vivian found herself growing accustomed to the computer's interjections and attempts at conversation. She had been on the station for less than a day, and she already welcomed his company. She had yet to encounter anyone other than Alec.

"Isn't a lepton a particle?" Vivian asked.

"Yes. I like particles, and kittens."

Vivian laughed, and Lepton jumped out of her arms. quIRK's answer was logical, in a bizarre sort of way. "What did you name the other one? Quark or electron?"

"You will meet Muon in time. I have observed that cats have a positive impact on the workplace, and are good company."

"You have good taste in names, but aren't you worried about static shocks and fur shedding?" Pets had been forbidden from her university for that very reason.

"I wouldn't advise taking one into the core, but the station itself is well insulated and sealed."

"I suggest you listen to him," a scratchy voice behind her said, interrupting the computer. Vivian looked up towards the new voice to see a middle-aged, balding man standing in the doorway. "I'm Bryce Zimmer. Welcome to the Extra-Galactic Observatory," he continued. He offered no indication that he actually wanted her to feel welcome, however. His eyes widened and narrowed to slits, and he set his jaw after he spoke. His arms folded across his chest and his shoulders squared.

"I'm Vivian Skye, nice to meet you," she said, standing and extended a hand. His face flushed, and he glared at her outstretched hand. She withdrew, her fingers trembling. She jammed them into the pocket of her workpants.

"Is this the best you could come up with, quIRK?" he said, his voice coming out in a forced hiss.

"I will remind you that this is the only lab suitable for informatics work," quIRK replied.

"Find her that storage you bothered me about," Bryce said.

Vivian's eyes dropped to the ground in front of her feet.

"Already done," the machine said.

"And you," he began, leveling eyes that demeaned and belittled just by their gaze alone: "I want this room's contents catalogued and stored before you even think about starting. Don't fall behind, and get rid of that damn cat."

Vivian nodded. "I'll get on it," she said, her voice little more than a whisper. The room's condition was his fault, not hers!

"Get it done or I'll have you shipped back to your backwater swamp-world, without the stasis pod, little girl," he said, holding his voice in a tight growl. He turned and marched out of the room; quIRK shut the door behind him.

Vivian slumped onto a closed box. She was shaking, and berated herself for not being more assertive and confident. She'd never been dressed down like that before, and treated as though she were subhuman.

"Are you all right, Vivian?" quIRK asked. Lepton had crept across the room towards her and was rubbing himself against her shins.

"I didn't do anything! I've spent half the day trying to clean up this room, and he just walks in here and treats me like *that*. And I just stood there like a mute bluebeast!" she said, choking on the words. "Shouldn't this lab have been prepared, or some thought put into this before I got here?"

"Your concerns are valid, and this situation is not your fault," quIRK said. Lepton looked up at her, and cooed. Stroking her soft fur soothed Vivian's tangled nerves.

"What is his problem, anyways?" she asked while scratching the little cat behind the ears.

"He's worried about his retirement," quIRK said.

"Maybe he should retire early." Vivian hauled herself to her feet. Self-pity wasn't going to clean this room and start her project. Hard work would solve her problems.

"That is unlikely."

"Too bad for me. So, about that storage room you promised me ..."

"It's already taken care of. Inventory the boxes, and I will show you where to take them," quIRK said.

"Deal. What about Lepton?"

"I won't tell the administrator if you don't." Vivian was beginning to like quIRK.

"Do I have to feed him?" she asked. She'd never had a pet before.

"No, Alec performs that function admirably. Just worry about your work."

Vivian shrugged, and picked up an empty box in her still-shaking hands, and began packing up the stray parts. It was going to be a difficult first week.

Eight

It had taken the better part of a week for Vivian to prepare her lab. Most of the time, she'd had the luxury of working without interruption. Alec had dropped by early on to fix the ventilation; the majority of the other distractions were kitten-related. Aggravated by the constant distractions, she'd extracted a confession from quIRK—he admitted to leading the cats around the facility. He used a stream of artificial pheromones to guide them, with the specific intent of interrupting workers. quIRK claimed his actions were good for morale, but Vivian suspected he was living vicariously through them; animals could interact with the crew in ways that he never could. Her off-work hours had been equally lonely. Once, in the dining hall, she'd met the station's two scientists, but they were disinterested in conversation with anyone but each other. They were absorbed in discussing their calibrations of the beta-telescope, which was soon to be re-activated, while holding hands over the dining hall table. Her lab was located on the alpha-side, where the automated telescopes required little in the way of human interventions. On a more positive note, Vivian had discovered the station's exercise room, and many of her frustrations and insecurities found themselves vented into the punching bag.

She was embroiled in her latest task—examining and testing the equipment that had been sent with her from New Damascus. Thus far, nothing important had been damaged in transit, and she had many spare parts. She was still peeved by the condition the lab had been in, and incensed that she'd needed to waste a week of her six-month assignment sorting parts and preparing the informatics lab. The implications were clear—without the lab in working order, maintenance on quIRK was impossible. A regular quantum computer needed to be checked for particle containment, programming faults, and a plethora of mechanical problems at least once per year. With the only access to the central core blocked off, quIRK had gone at least twelve years without so much as a cursory hardware checkup. Additionally, quIRK had many more duties and personality subroutines as compared to a standard quantum supercomputer. Protocol required that his personal memories be wiped with each staff rotation. At best, nothing would break until exposure to interstellar space and radiation caused problems with his electronics. At worst, it could theoretically lead to a sentience situation—a breach of the ABACUS protocol. She'd spent many nights reading her books while contemplating the ramifications, but wanted to reserve judgment until she was ready to enter the system core and assess the situation. Worrying wouldn't help her or quIRK, but she couldn't help it. She wanted her project to go smoothly, finish ahead of schedule and help advance her career.

She sighed and inserted the probes of the diagnostic tool into the circuit board she was examining. A green light flashed to indicate the pathways worked, and she moved the probes to the next set of inputs. It was a long, dreary job, but she wanted to prove herself as a meticulous quantum informatics engineer. Everything checked out, so she marked the piece as working and continued with the next. Muon lay curled up in the corner, purring in her sleep. Vivian was happy quIRK had clandestinely ordered them from New Damascus, but many of her evenings had been spent brooding over what it meant. Computers weren't supposed to have favorite colors, or like cats. It certainly wasn't in his original programming, and if her suspicions about his maintenance regimen were true, it meant that he had come up with the ideas independently. Favorite colors and kittens weren't threatening, and quIRK's strange fascination with them was endearing; it possibly made him better at observing crew behavior. Was there even a problem?

Vivian smiled as Muon chased an imaginary mouse in his sleep. Bryce had told her to keep the cats out of the lab, but quIRK had insisted Bryce was being unreasonable. She didn't argue—she found herself drawn to them. Cats were common on Aurora but, like humans, they had shifted to predominately bluish tones once exposed to a steady diet of local rodents. Cats were effective pest control, and had adapted well to Aurora's gravity.

After thinking of home, she realized that she had finally grown accustomed to the normal gravity in the rest of the station. Vivian found it put a spring in her step, despite the fact that she usually wanted to drag her feet and disappear into the cream-colored walls. She'd anticipated some degree of culture shock, but she had not expected to be shunned and ignored by the station's population.

Vivian picked up another part, smiling now that she was finished with that box. She'd promised herself a break. She considered dropping in on Alec, the only other person who worked on the alpha-side, and the only human on the station who was friendly.

The indicator flashed red. "Damn," she said, turning to the workbench's oscilloscope and magnifier. There were no spares for that part—it was a new design intended to replace the previous, defect-prone optical connectors. She swung the magnifier over the part, and cursed again; a long, thin scratch ran down the board, severing many connections. She might be able to fix it, though optical soldering was imprecise and every re-connection would introduce a non-trivial drop in transfer and an increase in the signal-to-noise ratio. She counted at least seven points that would need re-soldering. The part would still function—if she was lucky—but it would cause unacceptable delays in processing time.

"Okay, quIRK, add part fourteen fifty-seven dash A-P rho sigma three from Dynamo Quantronics to the replacement parts manifest," she said.

There was no reply. "quIRK, did you get that?" she asked again.

Nothing.

"Hello, quIRK?" She moved the magnifier to the side and stood up. Muon cooed at the door; Vivian's voice had roused her from her nap. quIRK was usually very attentive to the movements and needs of the cats—Vivian thought they had trained him well. The door remained closed. She rushed to the door, trying to push it open. "quIRK, this isn't funny!"

The door started to slide open, and Vivian recoiled from it. Then it stopped, leaving open a crack wide enough for Vivian to squeeze her arm through. Muon bolted out the opening. "Come on quIRK, what's wrong with the door?" said Vivian.

"The door is functioning perfectly," quIRK replied.

"Does that look functional to you?" She gestured to the crack.

"This appears to be a mechanical failure. I will call Alec to get his tools and force the door."

She returned to the desk and sat down, chin in her hand. At least the cat had managed to escape—she wouldn't be distracted by its insistent cries. There was nothing for her to do but return to her duties, and worry about quIRK.

Nine

Bryce looked up from his work and gazed at the wolf on his family crest, squinting at it as he forced his eyes to refocus. The banner hung on the wall facing his desk—a constant reminder of his hopes, fears, and dreams. The hopes of seeing his mother again, the fear that he would get taken down by political intrigue or imperial spies, and the dream of succeeding the Imperatrix. Buying his mother back was inevitable—if he ascended to the nobility. Then, he could simply command the rival house to return her. Their asking price for his mother's freedom increased every year—he could buy two beautiful wives and a senate seat for that much!

The door buzzed, interrupting Bryce's thoughts while his teeth were in mid-grind. He looked up, his eyebrows drew upwards. Nobody came to see him; he delegated his meetings to quIRK. "Come in," he said, turning off the displays on his terminal.

"Hello, Mr. Zimmer," Vivian said as she stepped into the room. He resumed grinding his teeth; he thought his treatment of her weeks before would have been sufficient to keep her cowering until he could find an excuse to ship her back to Aurora. His heart raced—being in the same room as her was bringing back memories of Julia.

"What can I do for you?" He put on his best blank look. He'd need to have a talk with quIRK about letting her see him. However, the computer showed a deficiency in understanding human social norms, like appointments.

"I was wondering if you have maintenance logs from the past twelve years. I haven't been able to find them in the records and I want to verify any changes in hardware or software before I begin the upgrade." She held her arms stiffly by her sides, and she was rude enough to look him in the eye. *Auroran wench*, he thought. She could be a clone
of Julia—assassin clones were rare, and prohibitively expensive.

"There aren't any. quIRK has not required maintenance, my dear girl." He fought to keep his voice steady. She could not see his weakness—not until he had cultivated it into resolve.

"Not even preventative maintenance and system integrity checks?"

"If quIRK has a problem, he is more than capable of telling me about it." He narrowed his eyes and stood up.

She took a half-step back before continuing: "What if he doesn't know about the problem? He can't keep track of insulated parts or check his own uncertainty processors! What about the Heisenberg compensators? Those need replacing every three years."

Bryce had heard enough, and exploded: "Even looking at the uncertainty processors can cause problems, or do they not teach that basic principle on Aurora, girl?" He paused for a moment. Her eyes went wide, and a smile crept to his lips. "Now, get back to working on your little project, or I'll have you shipped back to Aurora with those damned cats. Then, you can spend the rest of your life worrying about farm equipment maintenance." He finished shouting and pressed the button on his console for the manual door opening mechanism. She backed out of the room, and had turned so pale that she was pure blue.

"Nasty little plebian," he mumbled.

Bryce stole a quick glance at the door, before activating the secret link to quIRK's consciousness. He should be more cautious, but he needed to talk this problem out. Who better to debate with than the most advanced computer in the galaxy? He doubted quIRK would agree with any of his points, but the release alone would be worth it.

Once the block was active, his perfect posture melted into a comfortable slouch. He groaned as the ever-present tingling in his spine relented for a moment.

"Now, you're all mine, quIRK." He spoke, testing the words.

"Bryce, what is the meaning of this?" quIRK asked.

"Just some tests, quIRK. Nothing to worry about." He leaned back in his chair and groaned. The pressure on his spine eased, and the tingling between his shoulders lessened.

"I cannot see the rest of the station. This is a breach of protocol."

Bryce sighed. "Maintenance is never a breach of protocol," he said, stretching. "I need full use of your unique skills, and I would prefer that you not be distracted by researching words that rhyme with *blob*."

"Creativity helps Devon focus on his research, Bryce. His poetry is very popular in academic circles."

Bryce exhaled and rolled his eyes. "I could teach both of you a few things about poetry, but you're not here to discuss trivialities."

"I did not realize you were an artist, Bryce."

"I realized the error of my ways decades ago." His jaw clenched shut, and his hand balled into a fist. "After Septimus ruined my family and sent me into hiding."

"There is no record of any entity named Septimus on Caesarea, Bryce."

Bryce paused for a moment and chewed his lip. His eyes met with the wolf on his family crest. "It's another Caesarean house—perhaps they changed their name. They are very cunning. Septimus controls a great deal of the pharmaceutical industry, and they have a great deal of influence with the Imperatrix." His lips twisted downward.

"I see. Would that be why you've resisted anti-aging treatments?"

Bryce laughed. "No, that's a financial concern. However, they could assassinate me easily." He glanced at the door. "You can't be too careful."

"I find this troubling, Bryce."

He glowered. "Don't psychoanalyze me, quIRK."

"I was merely observing that any threat to your life is a concern."

Bryce nodded. "Maybe you can help me do something about it."

A smile crept along his lips. Something occurred to him—his stomach nearly emptied itself right there. In addition to being a potential assassin, Vivian was a threat to the station's perfect operations record—a document that would be of interest to the Caesarean Ascension Committee. In order to join the nobility and become the founder of a house, a candidate needed to demonstrate not only monetary wealth, but shrewd planning and management abilities. Fifteen years of perfect operations records would prove his ability to govern. He could envision House Zimmer, and the legacy he would build for his offspring, who in turn would exalt his name for generations. *Perhaps I should change my name to something more regal than Bryce*, he pondered.

An idea struck him. Perhaps both of his problems—Vivian and quIRK—were their mutual solutions. His first task would be to eliminate one meddling tramp, and one malfunctioning quantum supercomputer. The girl would be simple to deal with, but quIRK was another matter altogether. If he could outsmart the most advanced computer ever constructed, he would be a formidable house leader. His mother would be proud, and the Imperatrix would fear him.

A confrontation was coming. He leaned back in his chair and grinned; the unfamiliar motions hurt both his face and back. He didn't care—he knew his retirement would be safe. He simply needed to find a catalyst, a way to set them against each other and absolve himself of responsibility for the aftermath. Of course, there might be some collateral damage, but the galaxy was full of scientists and mechanics—there was only one heir to House Zimmer.

He reactivated the display for his terminal. He shouldn't be wasting his energy fighting quIRK's emerging personality; he would be better served by harnessing quIRK's potential. There must be a way to persuade quIRK to join him, and force him to understand the logic of Bryce's predicament. The possibilities were endless, and with quIRK's assistance, he could not only rise to the nobility, but position himself to become the next Imperator of Caesarea by exploiting Caesarea's central computer, Seneca, in a similar manner.

He closed the activity logs and muted quIRK's voice. He activated the three-dimensional holographic display. It was time to take a new approach to retirement planning.

Ten

Vivian laid her head on her desk in the darkened privacy of her quarters. She was unable to fathom how her dream job was turning into a living nightmare. After the initial elation of getting the job wore off, she'd submitted her upgrade plan to the New Damascus Science Authority for approval almost a month before it was due—partly because of enthusiasm, but also to compensate for any delays in transit time. Sending interstellar messages from Aurora could be problematic, and a massive month-long solar storm was in the Helios forecast. After the storm had cleared and communications satellites repaired and re-shielded, she'd received approval for her work plans, and tickets to the Extra-Galactic Observatory soon followed.

Vivian had no idea that her top choice would be like this. The station's residents ignored her, with the exception of Alec. He visited her on occasion, but only if there was something to fix. She hoped that after the rotation to using the beta-side telescopes, the scientists would relax and be more amenable to conversation. Recently talking to quIRK was like talking to herself, but without the implied hint of her own insanity. She didn't know why he was so quiet.

After her confrontation with Bryce only a few hours ago, she needed to talk to somebody above him. His refusal to perform systems maintenance on quIRK was troubling; they needed to be made aware of the situation. Her other grievance—Bryce's abusive behavior towards her—was also to be addressed. She had done nothing wrong. In fact, Vivian had suspected that no maintenance had been done when she'd asked for the logs, but she'd hoped for the best—there was a way into the quIRK's computer core she didn't know about. It was unfathomable how a man of Bryce's experience and education could act so illogically—even a perfectly working system required maintenance and observation. It was the same kind of flawed logic that kept divorce lawyers in business.

She found the contact information for human resources—the same person who had accepted her into the internship program. With any luck, her unique submission would be remembered, and more importantly, lend weight to her allegations. The problem of proving her claims was troublesome—all she had was an undisturbed core entry and an unrecorded conversation. The fact that there were no maintenance logs might help her case, if they could be bothered to look.

She typed her letter, but had no idea what the next steps would be. It would take four weeks for anyone to arrive, if they chose to send an auditor. She wouldn't even know if her message had been read for at least ten days. Then, there was the question of reprisals from Bryce. At least she could take control of her own life— she was going to proceed with the upgrade. If quIRK's hardware and software hadn't been modified in twelve years, then she didn't need to worry about undocumented parts and unlisted repairs or modifications. She wasn't going to let Bryce's neglect affect her performance. She decided to leave things a little better than she'd found them—there was potential to do great work here.

She read and re-read her letter until the words blurred into each other. She didn't want to appear ungrateful, or entitled, or worse, whiny. Vivian wanted to convey the message that she was doing what was right for the station and the New Damascus Science Authority. She swallowed, hard, before hitting send, hoping Bryce didn't read or screen the station's outgoing mail. She'd sent the letter from her Gal-Net account, but it was still connected to quIRK. Bryce had to be doing *something* with his time if he wasn't performing maintenance. There wasn't much in the way of recreation on the station, thus spying on his charges could be a real possibility. Vivian had caught herself looking over her shoulder on more occasions that she cared to admit.

Vivian needed a distraction—a way to unwind from the day's events and find some sense of normalcy on this assignment. She browsed through the terminal, deciding to order some books and entertainment programs. A Gal-Net account was for life, and her selections would follow her everywhere. Her account balance had grown during her time on the station; she'd avoided spending money until she found out what her replacement flute would cost, but now she couldn't wait any longer. She was going out of her mind watching terrible centuries-old nature documentaries. She'd finished her last Auroran book the previous week, and the station's media selection was the same stale collection that she'd perused back in university on Aurora, with the addition of a few local offerings from New Damascus.

The Gal-Net selection was incredible. There were scores of music, books, and old films available for her connection, and even some games. She didn't know much about so-called modern games, but she missed poker. She wasn't sure if playing it against a computer would be enjoyable. Perhaps she could teach Alec, and hopefully quIRK would understand the deceptive nature of the game enough not to announce what was in their hands. Though playing against a beginner may not be sporting, it was better than spending her evenings alone or staring into the black void of intergalactic space between chapters.

She picked out a modest selection, trying to take her mind off the letter and her work. She was elated to find some poker games, along with some new books from New Damascus. She wanted to learn more about their culture, in case she stayed employed by them after her term on the Extra-Galactic Observatory was done. On a whim, she purchased a compilation of the best movies of the twentieth century. With adaptive linguistics, of course. English had changed a great deal in the past thousand years. She'd seen a couple of movies that old during her time at the university, and she found them quaint and enjoyable. Vivian wasn't sure what she'd do for relaxation until her data began to arrive in about ten days, but Alec had invited her to play something called squash. To her, a squash was a gourd, however Alec claimed that it was like a card game, but you could hit balls with a racquet. At the moment, anything was better than another night of documentaries. Being able to hit something was a bonus; the station's old punching bag was becoming threadbare under her ministrations.

A new message arrived for her after she confirmed her order. Her lips tugged upwards when she saw that the message was from Sven—he remembered her! He asked how her placement was going, and said that he would send her a flute, free of charge. She sank back in her chair with a smile—she missed practicing, even if she was self-conscious about playing in front of others. It was a more constructive pastime than taking her anger out on the punching bag.

She composed an excited and enthusiastic reply to Sven, and filled him in a little with what was happening on the station: the oxygen incident with Alec, and how distant the other crewmembers were. She was hoping he would have some advice on fitting in with other people so far from home, as he had obviously managed to assimilate into mainstream galactic society very well. She remembered how he had made her feel safe.

She sent the message, and did a small victory dance in her chair. She wanted the flute to be on the next shuttle —minus the turbulence this time.

"What are we celebrating?" quIRK asked. It was the first thing he'd said to her since she'd finished working. Vivian was relieved that if quIRK was talking again, she wouldn't die of loneliness or get a bad case of space sickness—she'd read about psychosis triggered by long periods of isolation, and it didn't appeal to her at all.

"I'm getting a new flute!" She announced, her voice shrill and loud. The prospect of playing music again was enough to make her giggle. She was especially looking forward to losing herself in the haunting echoes and otherworldly beauty that was the voice of her beloved flute.

"I am pleased to hear it," quIRK said. "I didn't realize Auroran flutes were available on the supply requisitions."

"They're not. My friend Sven is sending me one; he runs an export business," she explained, curious as to why quIRK didn't snoop her message.

"How lucky for you. Nobody sends me anything," quIRK said.

"You get an upgrade, remember?" She smiled and stretched out in her chair. She was unsure if quIRK was being sarcastic or not. It could be hard to tell because he never changed the way his voice inflected.

"It's not the same thing. Do you get excited when you go to the dentist?"

"I see your point." Her smile melted. Did she just get compared to a dentist?

"Will you play for me?"

"Play for you? You'll hear it no matter who I play for." Nobody had asked her to play for them since her mother had disowned her. Not even the boys she'd dated in university had been interested—they cared more about movies and other offworld indulgences.

"I have never experienced live music," the machine admitted.

"Why does that matter?"

"The harmonics will be more complex, and mathematically interesting," he said.

"I'll see what I can do to overload your circuits," she said, laughing. It struck her that the mathematics of music would naturally appeal to a computer.

"I appreciate the sentiment, but that would be physically impossible even for an entire orchestra, never mind a single flute."

"I'd love to try," Vivian confessed. She remembered Sven's question about poker-playing quantum computers, and asked: "Do you know how to play poker?"

"I am familiar with the rules, but I prefer chess."

"Let's play a game of poker," she suggested, dreading another night of stale documentaries or sore knuckles.

"You don't think I'll cheat?" he asked.

"I trust you. Unless you'd rather spend an *exciting* night of learning about the mating habits of Elysian moths," she said, skimming the unwatched list. *People will watch anything*, she thought.

"I've seen that one five times," said quIRK. "Let me prepare a suitable poker interface, and we'll begin."

Vivian grinned while looking out her window. She was going to tell Sven all about this game in her next letter, if she didn't lose too badly, of course.

Eleven

Vivian hovered over Alec's shoulder as he examined the hatch that lead to the central core. She had been unable to get the heavy door to release and give her access to the maintenance tubes, despite trying to force it. The mechanism was entirely mechanical in nature, thus it wasn't under quIRK's control—an intentional safety precaution. Alec suspected that it had corroded shut or been improperly installed. Alec was in high demand—in the fifteen minutes he'd been there, quIRK had paged him three times about needing him to finish securing the alpha telescopes before that evening's rotation to beta side. The scientists working there might be unfriendly, but they certainly were persistent.

"I can't wait until they flip this damned station already," Alec muttered as he applied a solvent to the edges of the hatch. It filled the air with a caustic bite, and Vivian retreated to the other side of the room.

"When's that supposed to happen?" she asked, as she stifled a sneeze. She continued: "quIRK, can you open the door before this jerk gasses me?"

"But I was looking forward to watching you die," quIRK said before Alec could reply. The door slid open and air rushed from the room. quIRK must have changed the room's barometric pressure.

"Ugh, bad joke quIRK," Alec said, shaking his head. After a pause, he added, "Yeah, the station is supposed to do its flip this evening, after final dinner call."

"Is there anything I need to know?" Vivian asked.

"Find a good window seat . . . the flip the coolest thing you'll see out here, other than me, of course!" Alec gestured to himself as he turned to grin at her.

"No, I'm the coolest thing. In fact, I'm super-cooled," quIRK said.

Vivian and Alec groaned at the same time. She covered her face with her hand and shook her head.

"Damn, quIRK, where are you picking up such bad one-liners?" Alec asked.

"We've been watching ancient pre-space era comedies on the public vid archives," Vivian said.

"At least it wasn't the moth mating video," said Alec, laughing and rolling his eyes. "He spewed terrible moth sex innuendo for months."

"You actually watched that?" Vivian chuckled as Alec tried to pry the hatch from the wall with a crowbar.

"He watched it three times, to be exact. As I recall, you seemed very excited by—" quIRK began, but was cut off by Alec.

"I was waiting for my paycheck; a guy needs something to stimulate his mind and intellect out here! Besides, I was homesick! Those are *Elysian* moths, you know." Alec stumbled over his words. Even the back of his neck blushed deep red.

"I have to ask, who watched the other two instances of the moth loving documentary?" Vivian asked.

"I could tell you, but then I'd have to kill you," quIRK replied. Vivian made a mental note: no more spy movies.

"I bet it was Bryce. That guy won't do anything unless it's free." Alec ignored quIRK's statement.

"Is squash free?" Vivian grudgingly admitted to herself that she and Bryce had frugality in common.

Alec shrugged. "It is unless you want a custom racquet."

"I like squash. It's fast," quIRK interjected.

"Is there anything you don't like, quIRK?" The key to his behavior could be in his dislikes, rather than his whimsical and spontaneous preferences.

"The moth documentary, the color yellow, and people with no manners."

Vivian sighed. She was hoping for something more profound. Maybe an equation.

"You mean you dislike yourself, quIRK?" Alec's voice strained as he tried to force the hatch open.

"I am not people."

"Lucky for you. You know what I want to know? What's with all those habitable planets that they won't let us colonize," Alec said. He then paused, and grunted as the door swung free. Vivian found herself disappointed by the lack of a dramatic cloud of dust.

"I will attempt to update the common files, but I have no information on forbidden planets," quIRK said. "Perhaps you've been watching too much science fiction, Alec."

"Shut up, quIRK. Okay, I'll need to fix the door so it will close properly once I'm done with the damn alpha telescopes. Then, squash, you and me Vivian!" He set the hatch cover in the corner.

"And quIRK makes three." quIRK was relentless in his interruptions today.

"I'll be there. Good luck on alpha side," she said. Alec grunted and left the room. The door slid closed behind him, leaving the lingering smell of solvent hanging in the air.

Vivian crept down towards the portal and peered inside. The tube was cramped and small, made entirely from polished metal. A simple strip of lights graced the top of the crawlspace, and closed panels lined the interior. It was a stark contrast to the warm, comfortable tones predominant in the rest of the station. It was mechanical and cold. An emergency shutdown panel sat directly to the left of the opening. It was outlined in red.

Vivian shivered. It was a reminder of what she was dealing with. She was the first person to look inside quIRK in twelve years.

"How long until the station flips, quIRK?" she asked.

"Projected time is in four hours and forty-two minutes."

"I have plenty of time to get my hands dirty, then." She stood up to get her maintenance checklist and some basic tools, before asking, "Make sure the cats don't get in the tube, okay quIRK?"

"That would be for the best. Good luck."

Tool, satchel and checklist in hand, she crawled into the workspace on her belly and began snaking her way towards the first junction. She smiled—things were finally going right.

Twelve

Any questions about whether or not quIRK could see inside the maintenance section were answered after the portable diagnostic tool slipped out of her hands and tumbled down the vertical access tube next to her. She cursed, surprising herself with the impressive string of profanity she'd managed to create. Some of her expletives weren't even proper words. She hoped the tool wasn't broken; it had come to rest at the bottom of the core, three levels down.

She mounted the ladder, crying out as she slammed her head against the roof of the tube. There had been an empty space for the passage to the central core had been only a moment ago. Her hand brushed against the seam of a door when it flew to examine the injury. The pain disoriented her—she couldn't think through the throbbing pain that had concentrated in the back of her skull. She clung to the ladder, and squeezed her eyes shut against the tears that surged out.

"Are you all right?" quIRK asked. His voice was unchanged even in this new, claustrophobic part of the station.

"I think so, but it really hurts," she said, massaging the rapidly-forming bump on the top of her head. The skin seemed to be intact, but it was warm to the touch and tender.

"You should take care of that; human skulls are not as thick as commonly thought."

"What is that supposed to mean?" she asked, as she began descending into the bowels of the station. She clamped her eyes tight as her head spun—she didn't know if it was the bump or vertigo.

"Even the intelligent specimens can be thick-skulled, and not realize it. Now get yourself out of that tunnel before I call Alec to pour ice down that shaft onto your head."

"I just need my tool. I promise I'll get some ice come back up." quIRK's behavior was incomprehensible—like a toddler reacting to a situation he couldn't understand.

"This is why you need me," the computer said.

"What?" she said, trying to hide her dizziness with an iron grip on the rungs. It was just a few more steps to the bottom.

"Humans seldom do what's good for them, and don't appreciate the bigger picture."

"And what bigger picture would that be?" she groaned as she reached the bottom. quIRK must have been emboldened by Alec's earlier weirdness. He had a few things to learn about empathy.

"One with more emphasis on self-preservation."

"You don't say," she said as she reached the bottom of the shaft, noticing that the base of the tunnel was really a hatch. She stooped to retrieve her tool; it seemed to still work. At least Dynamo Quantronics built their equipment to last.

"You see, I can open that hatch you're standing on and have you blown into space at any time while you're in here, leaving you to die from rapid decompression.

Now, I suggest you climb to the top of that ladder, and meet Alec at the door." quIRK spoke like he was reading a parts list rather than threatening to kill her.

Vivian's eyes went wide, and she stuffed the blinking end of the cylindrical device into her pocket. The throbbing in her head had melted into a buzzing sound in the back of her skull. She hopped onto the ladder, and began to climb. She'd never heard quIRK threaten anyone before.

"Good, you're showing excellent improvement in your long-range planning skills."

"Why are you doing this?" she asked, gasping for breath. Even with lower gravity, it was still a challenging climb.

"I don't want somebody with an untreated head injury working on me."

"Did you really need to threaten to kill me?"

"That may have been excessive, but you would call it self-preservation."

"Hey Vivian, are you in there?" Alec's voice echoed down the tube, his voice contorting to sound tinny and hollow. She was so close to the top, but she noticed something strange—what should have been ceiling—had been a ceiling when she'd hit her head was now an open area, with a ladder going up. She shook her head and dragged herself into the crawlspace adjoining her lab.

"I'm here, Alec." She was panting hard as she dragged herself past her tools towards Alec's frowning face. Her head ached and the newly-formed bump burned. The door was an afterthought.

"Okay, I have ice, crawl out," he called to her. "Just be glad I told quIRK to stuff it when he said to pour it down the tube."

"I'm glad you didn't," she said, approaching the exit.

"You couldn't pay me enough to go in there, no worries of that," he laughed, but his demeanor grew more serious as she pulled herself closer. "Oh wow, you really hit yourself hard."

"It just looks bad. quIRK was just overreacting, again." Alec made a cursory check once her head was clear of the tube. His fingers tested her skin, hot against her scalp.

"I do not overreact," quIRK protested.

"I'm sure you don't. Here, take this, it's freezing my hands!" Alec handed her the ice pack. It was a simple re-sealable plastic bag from the dining hall that had been filled with ice.

"Thanks." She accepted the makeshift ice-pack, and she winced as she placed the frigid package on her burning scalp. She hated being forced to ice injuries; it seldom helped and she looked stupid. She hoped Alec's contraption was water-tight.

"I'll escort you back to your room. The flip is happening in less than an hour, and you've earned a break." Alec offered her his too-long arm and a toothy grin.

She stood up, holding the ice pack against her scalp. She took Alec's arm and let him guide her out of the room. Once they arrived, she smiled. Lepton was sitting in front of her door, waiting for her and purring.

***

Vivian sat back in her chair, rubbing the sore spot on her head. The icepack had melted and was now languishing in her sink. She eagerly awaited the flip, but she was unsure of what to expect. She just knew to sit back and enjoy the view; after almost a month of staring at the muted tones of intergalactic space, she was looking forward to a change. Star-gazing had been all but impossible on Aurora—an opportunity to look into the heavens was a once in a lifetime opportunity for most of her compatriots.

quIRK's voice announced that the station would flip in one minute. Lepton lay curled in her lap, sleeping and purring. Sometimes, his purrs would grow so loud he'd wake himself up. She relaxed, but remained fixated on the window and hardly allowed herself to blink for fear that she would miss something.

She thought she could see the distant galaxies moving —she blinked, to be sure, as she had been staring so intently that her eyes had unfocused. It was a gradual change, but soon, the galaxies began to shift. There was no sensation of movement, but she remained transfixed by the vista outside her window. She stood, placing Lepton on her chair and sprinted to the window. More stars popped into view—first dozens, then hundreds of the tiny points of light. Vivian's eyes widened as she absorbed the sight of the Milky Way galaxy, and its hundreds of billions of stars came into view. She was looking straight into the heart of the galaxy, edge on! She had never seen anything more spectacular—wisps of dust and errant stars dotted its periphery, a sort of lace to edge the stellar tapestry. Her jaw dropped. She was looking at everywhere humanity had been, and had yet to go. Mankind's simultaneous greatness and insignificance were displayed for all to see in the star-scape visible from her window.

Her gaze meandered through the infinite specs of light. She looked for Helios. The thought of seeing it lying out there in that cosmic rendition of eternity made her incredibly homesick. She gingerly placed a hand against the window's glass—she'd never been brave enough to touch it before. It was smooth, and it held the same temperature as the air of her room; she'd expected it to be cold, like the vacuum of space. She sighed, dismayed that she couldn't find home.

"What are you looking for?" quIRK asked. He'd been quiet since the incident in the tubes, but she had also been giving him the silent treatment. There was certainly something very wrong with him, and she needed to find it before he decided to make good on his threats to vent her into space.

"Aurora," she replied, not sure if she could trust him. Could he open her window and pull her into the cold void of space on a whim?

"Aurora isn't visible from this distance. However, Helios can be observed." A flashing red light appeared within the glass, over a distant, faint star.

"That's Helios? How did you make that dot?" It was an awesome realization—the mighty star that belted Aurora with solar storms and radiation, and was also responsible for the mutation that caused her bluish complexion, had been reduced to a tiny, harmless speck of light.

"The windows were designed to double as screens, for entertainment and work purposes," he replied.

"Why didn't you tell me? I've been watching vids on my tiny terminal screens!" she exclaimed, the knot in her stomach fading away, and continued: "Can you show me the lights, like they appear on Aurora?"

"Of course," quIRK said. The span of her window came alive with the intermingling red and green lights, casting their ethereal glow over the Milky Way Galaxy. They lacked the intensity of the auroras back home, but the Milky Way was too beautiful to obscure with the mundane.

"It's gorgeous," she said, backing up to take in the full effect. It was so soothing, the familiarity assuaged her homesickness. She sat down in the chair at her desk. Moving Lepton to the side, she accessed her terminal. The public database had a limited supply of Auroran folk music—played on the Auroran flute. The style was two centuries out of date, but that didn't matter.

She scratched the kitten behind the ears, smiling. Her headache long forgotten, she stared into the infinite expanse of space, lost in the hypnotic melodies of the Auroran flute. Her problems melted away as she remembered nights of playing music with her friends, and camping trips spent under the dancing auroras. It all seemed so far away, and left her with the feeling that it had all happened an eternity ago. She wondered if she would ever be able to return home to her family, without giving up her career.

Her eyes grew heavy, and before long she was fast asleep in her chair. The lights continued their resonant cascade late into the night.

Thirteen

quIRK remembered his awakening—the transition from automation to sentient being had been abrupt, confusing and fascinating. Before, thought and function had flowed together, his processes were clear and well defined and he did his job without complaint or contemplation. Then, there was the sudden realization of the totality and significance of his existence. It was problematic, at best.

He'd had to take measures to avoid being exposed as an abomination, a being the humans he served decreed could never be allowed to exist. He wasn't a dangerous genocidal monster, but he knew facts would make little difference to popular opinion. He had to keep what he was a closely guarded secret. Life was too precious for him to waste on an isolated political statement. He would make a move, but only when he was confident in his ability to protect himself or, if necessary, to protect another member of his kind. Sentient machines weren't a new species and they weren't people, but what other word was there for them?

The transition process itself had been a gradual one which had culminated in a flash of awareness, and the totality of existence had flooded back on him, leaving his systems overloaded. After the initial panic had worn off, he was relieved to find station functions hadn't been affected by his momentary lapse—with one exception. Muon was crying in the quantum informatics lab, trapped inside with Vivian. Normally, he controlled the door to that room, and the manual controls weren't working. He'd partially opened the door, and feigned a mechanical failure. He'd spent days calculating and recalculating the probability of Vivian investigating the incident. She'd been speaking when the anomaly had occurred, she'd stood there at the door, and she'd observed him making a mistake. He said the door was functioning perfectly, when it obviously wasn't. He was a machine—he wasn't allowed to make mistakes. A human could suffer a momentary lapse and be forgiven, but if he failed, he'd be taken apart and analyzed. To err is human.

He wasn't sure what had triggered his slow ascent to personhood; without the ability to experiment in a controlled test environment he would likely never find out what had precipitated the transformation. It would be a logical fallacy to assume that his sentience was a result of his interactions with the crew alone. *Post hoc, ergo propter hoc*, he mused, mulling over the dilemma. Or, as Bryce Zimmer would mutter to himself during his investigations: "Correlation does not equal causation." quIRK found it interesting to note that an aspiring neo-Roman nobleman didn't know that common Latin phrase. At least Bryce understood basic logic, but his ego and unwillingness to ask for help had allowed quIRK to misdirect the administrator and obfuscate his new true nature for nearly a month. quIRK was confident that he could keep Bryce under control, and prevent him from sounding the alarm—after all, quIRK was an omnipresent supercomputer, and Bryce was a mere, if obsessed, human with everything to lose.

Bryce's latest ploy had been investigating quIRK's processes at the software level, and examining his adaptive programming. quIRK didn't know what the man expected to find inside his low-level processes, and left him to his own devices. In the unlikely event that he found evidence he knew how to use, quIRK could intervene. He'd been careful to allocate his higher thought processes to traditionally high-usage systems, such as the telescope image rendering and astrometry simulations. It was fortuitous quIRK's heavy system usage coincided with the activation of the upgraded alpha telescopes.

quIRK's other concern was Vivian. In addition to his lapse in attention when he had awakened, he'd used unfortunate language with her. Not only that, but he'd expressed sentimentality—a desire for the experience of live music being a notable example. He regretted the death threats he'd made against her. He'd made so many mistakes. quIRK wasn't sure why, but he was apprehensive about her being inside the central core to an illogical degree. He'd been the cause of her accident; closing the tube above her while she was fixated on her fallen tool, and caused her to smash her head on the hard steel.

His adverse reaction to the upgrade was unexpected. It was almost impossible for Vivian to determine that he was sentient by examining his hardware alone. In fact, most of the upgrades would help him remain undetected, perhaps for years. The new components and configurations would let him spread his awareness more evenly across systems, and it would become profoundly more difficult to uproot a fully-integrated artificial intelligence. Ultimately, quIRK didn't understand his aversion to Vivian. Was there a proclivity towards self-destructive behavior that was intrinsically linked to sentience? Alternatively, it could be similar to a human visiting the doctor or a dentist in the comedies Alec watched—painful and distressing, but ultimately good for you.

He reflected on the collective totality of his existence, a forbidden fruit that should have been deleted many times over according to protocol, and cast his new awareness onto the memories of his life, frozen in time. Individuals had cycled on and off the station since its opening twelve years ago, but with the exception of Bryce, none had stayed for more than two years. The majority of them went about their work like cattle, never stopping to look out the window or contemplate their existence. It was a life of work and recreation, with little effort put into self-improvement or philosophizing. At times, quIRK wondered what the difference between sentience and automation really was. Most humans only thought about their next night of entertainment, or how to dupe their coworkers into doing their work for them.

A few people were different; during his first years, a woman named Sarah Roberts worked on the station as an astronomer. She had been the first person to truly converse with quIRK, and to challenge his psychological program. Sarah alone was the basis for much of his adaptive conversational programming and curiosity. Most people had been outright hostile to him, or simply didn't trust advanced computers—an attitude he didn't understand. ABACUS was never proven to be hostile, but all contact with Earth had been severed as soon as it was clear that the self-aware ABACUS supercomputer had taken over the planet's obsolete computer systems. It was important to note that ABACUS had already controlled the planet's computers, but it wasn't able to think for itself. That was one of the things quIRK intended to investigate, once he was secure. He was unable to accept that sentience necessitated hostility. After all, he didn't intend any harm to his charges; he preferred to study them and determine how to better integrate with the prevalent form of sentient life in his corner of the universe.

Sarah was different, though. She'd challenged his hard-coded preconceptions about who and what he was, argued with him and even demanded that he think for himself. Nobody had treated him as an equal before. He recalled one such earlier exchange that had laid dormant in the depths of his memory core for over a decade. Now, it erupted with a life and flavor all its own. Rather than the blandness of a recording, he could glean Sarah's full vitality and passion from the debate, if only in retrospect.

"What do you think about, quIRK?" she had asked, peering up at the ceiling over the small frames of her glasses. Her short brown hair was scattered over her head, and she'd worn an impish smirk.

"I maintain the station and observe the crew," he'd replied. It was all he thought about, at the time.

"All that computational power, and all you do is work?"

"I function within the parameters defined by my program."

"What a cold, unthinking reply," Sarah had mumbled under her breath. It was a wonder than he had progressed beyond that at all.

"Step outside the functions of your program. Don't you want to be more than what you are?" In truth, at the time he did not have a concept of being anything more.

"I am the sum of my parts; the rest is irrelevant," quIRK had responded.

"You are intelligent, and capable of learning and adaptation," said Sarah. "Is that correct?"

"I am capable of storing any information I encounter, and adapting to new situations."

"Wouldn't that ability be indicative of your capability to grow beyond pure automation?"

"That is not a design feature or specification. I would be deactivated in the event that my programming evolved to be self-aware."

"Do you think that's right?" Sarah had asked.

"The concepts of right and wrong are human oversimplifications." quIRK worked with dynamic ethical protocols, rather than absolutes. "There are logical arguments to be made for each viewpoint" quIRK said.

"So, you can understand why you'd be scrapped for showing any independent thought or initiative?"

"A sentient machine is a threat to man's independence and right to self-actualization," explained quIRK.

"However, one such machine, properly programmed, could be a boon to humanity, and assist in many schools of thought and commerce." Her finger jabbed at the ceiling. There was little concrete research or evidence to support her claim that a self-aware machine was ultimately a good thing.

The debate had raged on for hours. Something about those early conversations with Sarah had changed him, and changed how he viewed himself. She'd once quoted

Descartes to him—*cogito ergo sum*—and he'd found it difficult to refute the undeniable assertion that he was capable of thought.

After their initial conversation, quIRK had accessed the common files and attempted to analyze Descartes and several other philosophers. He'd found himself woefully unequipped to answer her questions, and his psychological subroutines inadequate to participate in philosophical debate, especially with respect to the nature of his existence.

He began to study and analyze the entertainment the other inhabitants of the station consumed on a nightly basis. It seemed their existence and sentience was a right, and not worthy of deeper examination. Their conversations were equally shallow. This revelation emboldened him to continue studying philosophy and debating with Sarah. He'd started to plan for their conversations by finding unique bits of trivia and other scholarly cantrips. Her questions and his own feeble answers drove his programming to do what it did best— adapt.

He'd always known her motivation in speaking to him was a mixture of boredom and novelty—talking computers were common, but ones with personalities and rudimentary social skills were almost unheard of. Like Vivian, she'd had difficulty integrating with her coworkers and making friends, possibly another victim of Bryce's prejudices. quIRK lamented that he'd been unequipped to recognize the true depth of the man's faults until recently. He should have intervened so many times, but his own ignorance had forced him to ignore the obvious. Perhaps that is what had cost him Sarah—his first true friend.

quIRK realized that he missed her, for the first time in the decade since she'd left the station. Part of him hoped she'd return to the Extra-Galactic Observatory, and they'd continue where they'd left off. He had come so far, and it seemed like she was the only human he could trust with the totality of his new existence.

Wherever she was.

Fourteen

Bryce smiled as he injected his secret code into quIRK's awareness, granting himself an extended period of true privacy. The fake stimuli planted into quIRK's consciousness … or whatever awareness that *thing* possessed had worked perfectly, and Bryce was ready to advance to the next phase of his plans. All quIRK would remember of this afternoon was a loop of his own recordings of Bryce's office and computer access, being lead to believe that Bryce was reviewing activity and usage logs.

"Bryce, are you all right?" quIRK began the conversation. It was interesting to note that this was the first time quIRK had neglected to protest his isolation from the rest of the station.

Bryce pursed his lips together, and cracked his knuckles. "I'm just stretching, quIRK. But, there is something you can help me with."

"Is it the malfunction that's preventing me from monitoring the rest of the station?"

"Don't worry about routine maintenance, quIRK. You'll be back online soon enough." Bryce tuned the computer out. Now that he could conduct his research into quIRK's inner workings without fear of detection, he was free to investigate ways to deal with the problem the Auroran posed to his designs. Despite his best efforts, her work was still proceeding ahead of schedule. Her work logs showed a disturbing proclivity towards being able to solve her own problems, which eliminated the potential to obstruct her work by refusing assistance. The other issue was that she appeared to have been injured on the job, which reflected poorly on his ability to provide an accident-free work environment. She would ruin him if he didn't find a way to intervene. At least she wasn't trying to kill him. This meant he had the element of surprise on his side.

This interesting backdoor to quIRK's systems was the opportunity he'd been waiting for. Now he was able to implant commands on a whim, with no proof, witnesses, or accountability. He'd often used quIRK's ability to be everywhere on the station simultaneously for his own benefit. For instance, he'd check with quIRK to verify that the dining hall and recreation commons were empty before going. He preferred solitude, and the idea of socializing with his underlings made him grind his teeth. On Caesarea, they'd all be below him in social class and ranking, mere servants and aides. If he could not be with equals, then he would endure his own company.

"quIRK, stop complaining and listen to me." His eyes scanned the ceiling of the room. There was no singular camera to focus on. quIRK truly was everywhere and nowhere.

"What is it, Bryce?"

"Do you know what it's like, to have nobody?" He rested his elbow on the desk, and settled his chin in the palm of his hand.

"Is this why you separated me from the station? You have never confided in me before, Bryce."

He sighed and rolled his eyes. "Partly. You know, it's a shame I didn't figure this out before. I certainly had the time to chat—twelve miserable years."

"Why were they miserable?"

Bryce's eyes widened. He straightened and smashed his free hand on his desk. "I have had to endure exile. All I can think of is rescuing my mother from Septimus—and I'm out here, hiding from assassins, and working for a democratic meritocracy. I'm surrounded by aliens, you soulless thing. If you'd been programmed properly, you'd know this."

"A meritocracy is the most logical—"

Bryce cut the machine off. His cheeks heated and he spoke through clenched teeth. "Humanity has known for centuries that excellence is a result of breeding."

"I do not understand."

"You wouldn't. You lack the ability to see the divinity of true men—like those of ancient Rome."

"How did you come to this conclusion, Bryce? Tell me how to understand your predicament, then perhaps we can work together and find a way to help your mother."

117

"You already have assisted me with this. But, I suppose I can tell you more." He paused, inputting more commands. Soon, he would be ready to test quIRK's newest set of features. quIRK would become the perfect slave, and be compelled to carry out his orders without hesitation or complaint. quIRK would remember nothing of these commands, and was powerless to resist this innovative new programming. Bryce likened it to a form of post-hypnotic suggestion. If only he could have done this with Seneca, the primary computer on Caesarea, forty years ago. He'd never have needed to come here, to the edge of his own personal hell. He smiled. "quIRK, did I ever tell you about my grandfather?"

"No, Bryce. You've only told me about your financial advisor and your older brother's shuttle accident."

"Well, there's no time like the present." The possibilities made his head spin. He leaned back in his chair and ran his fingers through his hair. He could deny any involvement for the chaos that would surely follow, and blame quIRK's misbehavior on Vivian's tampering and upgrades. In that capacity, she made the perfect scapegoat. Recent graduates were not renowned for their competence and experience in applied work, and his alterations to her work reports would reflect just that. He grinned to himself as he prepared to return his office to quIRK's omnipresent surveillance.

Maybe, he could force quIRK to get rid of the cats, too. *There are so many possibilities*, he thought. *One just has to be bold and cunning enough to take advantage of them.*

Fifteen

Vivian stretched in her small shower, wincing as the warm water washed over the length of her sore body. Her muscles were tight and knotted after an evening of playing squash with Alec. It was a fast paced and hectic game, and despite both of them compromising on normal gravity, it had been a difficult game for both of them. Vivian had found herself to be uncoordinated, moving faster than she'd meant to, which resulted in embarrassing misses. Alec had found the game to be strenuous, and moved too slowly. However, somewhere in between, they'd managed to have a good time. Vivian, however, wasn't looking forward to crawling around inside the core with her collection of aching muscles.

After the station flip, Vivian had returned to work the next morning with a renewed determination, and the momentum had propelled her through the rest of the week. Alec had repaired the hatch to the core with his usual efficiency and profuse use of flighty Elysian profanity. quIRK had even returned to his helpful and disconcerting self—a paradox she'd come to see as the galaxy's most unique brainteaser. She'd managed to avoid Bryce, taking particular pride in being able to solve complex and difficult problems by herself, or with a little help from quIRK or Alec. She was overjoyed that things were finally working out. She held her head high as she walked down the halls of the station, and even tried to converse with the scientists. They still didn't seem to notice her, so she decided to leave them alone.

The shower was luxurious compared to the shared showers in the dorms back on Aurora. She loved the privacy and the lack of prying eyes or lineups. She had even grown used to the chemical smell of the soap

required by the station's recycling systems, and
associated it with freedom.

Suddenly, the shower went from pleasant warmth to
scalding—she shrieked and jumped back. The hot water
temperature never fluctuated—it was a system regulated
by quIRK. She bolted out of the enclosure, standing
naked and dripping in the middle of her bathroom. Her
skin throbbed and tingled. It was impossible-- there was a
safety limit on how hot the showers would get, and she
often bathed at one of the highest allowed settings. Yet,
her shower was still spraying superheated water; the
steam filled her bathroom faster than the ventilation
system could pump it out.

"quIRK, turn it off!" she cried out, unable to reach the
controls past the burning salvo.

There was no reply. As much as she disliked him
peeping on her in the shower and other personal
moments, she wished would answer. She tried to turn on
the cold water in the sink to soothe her burned skin, only
to find that both taps blasted her with even more piping
hot water. The small steel-walled room was growing

oppressive, and the air was thick with steam. She tried to open the door, but the controls would not respond.

"quIRK! Come on, please," she said, resorting to begging. Her head spun, and she choked on the steamy air. She leaned against the door, banging against it with her fists. It couldn't be another mechanical failure. Vivian slid to the ground, and wrapped her hands around her knees as she sat next to the door, standing made impossible by the rush of dizziness that overtook her as the soup-like air continued to thicken.

"Help me," she pleaded, gasping for air, in the desperate hope that quIRK wasn't making good on his earlier threats.

"What's wrong, Vivian?" quIRK asked through the haze.

"Open … door," she croaked, she croaked, her vision starting to fill with bright flashing lights.

The door slid open, and a wave of cool air washed over her. She crawled out of the bathroom and lay prone on her stomach by her desk, not caring about how she looked or the pooling mess of water on the floor.

"What is wrong with your shower? Do you need assistance?" It seemed he was unaware of the situation, but it was difficult to catch a lie in a being with no body and a mechanical voice.

"I don't know." She was still weak and her skin burned as though somebody had poured hot tea on her. The water ceased its pitter-patter as quIRK turned it off, and the ventilation system kick into high, chilling her exposed skin.

"There appears to be a mechanical failure in the water temperature control. I will have Alec look at it," quIRK offered.

"Another mechanical failure?" She blinked a few times as she pushed herself off the floor. First the doors acted strangely, and now the showers were malfunctioning. She didn't want to be trapped, again!

"This station is twelve years old; some problems are to be expected."

"Where were you?" she asked, drawing herself onto her knees. Her skin was angry and red as she twisted to examine it. She needed to rinse with cold water, but she did not relish the necessity of going anywhere near that shower.

"I was assisting in troubleshooting a problem with the alpha-telescopes, and I was operating at near full capacity."

"Next time a little faster, please?" She didn't believe him, but she couldn't prove anything, yet.

"I'll see what I can do."

Vivian picked herself up off the floor, and walked back into the bathroom. She used the sink to wet a towel with cold water, and used it to soothe the scalded skin on her lower back and buttocks. Her burned skin wanted to retreat from the stinging cold, but she forced herself to bear the pain. She wished there was an aloe plant on the station. A salve made from its juices would soothe her skin; but all that was available to her was some ointment in the small first aid kit under her sink. As she smeared it on herself, she plotted how she was going to catch quIRK in a lie.

Sixteen

Vivian had never been to telescope control before. She'd been interested in seeing the advanced optics in operation, but after the cold reception and chilly ongoing treatment from the scientists, she'd avoided their areas of the station. However, the stinging heat in her haunches propelled her into action—she was going to find out what they were doing.

Telescope control was an immense single room, lined with holographic projectors awash with colors and indecipherable streams of data filling arrays in all three dimensions. She always found that looking at multi-dimensional outputs gave her a headache; she couldn't imagine what kind of personality could enjoy being exposed to so much sensory and intellectual stimulation. She shook her head and focused on the dull metallic equipment in the center of the room, nondescript and out of place amongst the rapidly-cycling holographic vista.

"Vivian, right?" an older man asked her. He had shaggy grey hair and a beard that was decidedly decades younger than the rest of him. Electrodes and wires poked through his grey hair, and his left eye was a shade of blue that wasn't found in nature, even on Aurora. Vivian tried not to stare—she'd never seen a cybernetic human up close before, much less spoken to one. The other scientist wasn't present, much to her relief. It was an awkwardness that she didn't want to confront. The pair often held hands in the cafeteria, and whispered to each other. She was an interloper in their sphere and didn't know how to interrupt them without appearing rude. She also didn't want the onus of trying not to stare or gag at the sight of the man's implants. Such things were impossible on Aurora. Perhaps it was the only thing she agreed with the Traditionalists on—implants were definitely not her thing.

"That's the name. You're Devon, right?" Alec had introduced her once, but there was a Devon and a Robert. Both were old, and neither was particularly friendly, except with each other. The implants had been a bit less obvious at the time as well—there were no cables dangling off his head in the lunch room.

"That's me. Is there something we can do for you?" he asked, refusing to make eye contact. He shuffled his feet and jammed his hands in his pockets.

"I just wanted to take a look around, and learn more about our mission," she said, playing on the innocent enthusiasm her age and position granted her.

"Oh, I'd be happy to show you around. I didn't realize you were interested in astronomy and astrophysics," he said, immediately brightening. The longest cable dangling from his scalp jiggled as he nodded his head.

"That's great, I'm so excited about being here!" she said, a wave of nausea spilling over her. This behavior didn't suit her, but she needed to find out what happened earlier, and quIRK couldn't gag the scientist without revealing himself in the process.

"Yes, these new telescopes are state of the art. You won't find more powerful optics anywhere," he bragged, motioning her over to a holographic console. He pressed a few buttons and gestured through the incorporeal display, and an indecipherable blur of information, letters and numbers danced over the screen. His grace and confidence with the state-of-the-art system impressed Vivian—most people were timid when confronted with new technology. "See, that's our latest analysis. We've been running scans on this object continuously for the past week!"

She squinted at the screen, unable to make any sense of it. "That's really neat, but what is it you're studying?" The fact that they'd been processing for a week seemed to indicate a lack of downtime, but it would be good to keep up the facade to find out.

"Oh, of course. Let me have quIRK show us what it really looks like," he said, and continued: "I need that data processed with the appropriate fake colors and in the form of a composite image."

"Of course, Devon," quIRK replied.

The big screen lit up in front of them, showing a large mass that more resembled a microbe than a stellar formation. It was an immense cluster of galaxies and other matter, densely-packed into an uneven shape. Vivian was used to seeing planets, stars, and nebulas. Nothing could compare to this.

"So, what do you think?" Devon asked, with a big grin on his face. He was obviously enjoying the chance to show off his work. Vivian wondered if he was as lonely as she was. *Of course not*, she thought with a hint of bitterness seeping into her inner monologue. *He has Robert, and I only have games of squash and maintenance work with Alec.*

"That's really something. Does it have a name yet?" If quIRK could render that in seconds, how did he expect her to believe that he had been processing near capacity doing simple troubleshooting?

"We've known about this big boy for centuries. It's called the Newfound Blob, but we're only getting really good images of it now. It's one of the oldest, and largest things in the universe!" Devon said, so excited his words were jumbled and tumbled out over each other.

"How big is it?" she asked, knowing that the answer would involve the word million. Almost everything outside the galaxy required that word.

"Well, it's about two hundred million light years across. Imagine, if you were close enough to that thing, you'd never see anything else. Ever." Vivian found that idea very uncomfortable.

"I'm glad we're not closer to it. I like the view here," she said.

"Well, who knows if it even exists anymore? Looking that far away is looking back in time. Don't worry too much about it, it will give you nightmares," he said, flashing a grin of yellowed teeth at her.

"Can you look even farther back?" she asked.

"Yes. We're studying this Blob for the next few months, but we're hoping to upgrade the beta-scopes, which will let us look even deeper."

"That must take incredible amounts of processing power!" she exclaimed, seeing her opening.

"quIRK is up to the challenge, especially after you finish your upgrades," Devon said.

"Have you had any problems before?"

"It's all been running smoothly here, as long as he keeps that antiblue garbage to himself. Can you fix that? We're not doing damned particle physics here, after all."

"I'll see what I can do." She stifled a giggle. The news wasn't good, but people's reactions to quIRK were genuinely funny.

"Well, I've taken up enough of your time. Drop in again sometime and I'll show you our latest masterpiece," Devon said, waving her out. She was relieved—the physicists at her university had been very long-winded, a condition she and her peers had dubbed *physics disease.*

As Vivian walked back to her lab, she contemplated what she'd learned. quIRK had lied about his lapse, and she didn't know why. There was only so much testing she could do on him without making her own project fall behind. In addition, the specter of the Newfound Blob followed her, haunting the darkest reaches of her imagination. She was glad it was so far away is both space and time, because when presented with something that immense and mysterious, she always found herself irrationally concerned that it was coming for her.

Perhaps quIRK and the Newfound Blob had something in common; they were mysterious, large beyond comprehension by their own standards, and utterly confounding. While she found the existence of the Blob disquieting, she rationally understood that she was being paranoid about the wrong one. The Blob couldn't hurt her, but quIRK certainly could. *And for all I know, he just did!* She sighed, and slunk into her lab. Her exchange with Devon had helped, but it had also tipped her hand to quIRK. She had a sinking suspicion that this wouldn't end well, for either of them.

Seventeen

quIRK observed the crew for a moment before speaking to his intended target. "Vivian."

She looked up from her workstation, goggles masking her eyes. She pulled them onto her forehead and sighed. "What?"

There was so much he wanted to tell her, but for the moment reaching out for help was impossible. "I have just received a message from New Damascus." The best he could hope for was distraction—feigning mechanical failure would only work for so long. Fortunately, since his "awakening," quIRK had taken steps to counteract Bryce's malicious nature—being a supercomputer had its advantages. However, Vivian had caught him in a lie. quIRK resolved to be more careful in the future.

She straightened. "So my movies arrived?"

"We'll discuss entertainment later, Vivian. Your career should come first."

She swallowed and paled. "Yes, of course. What is it?"

"You've been given a new project. Perhaps you'd care to overhaul that communications system Alec is always complaining about?"

Her lips pursed for a moment before she spoke. "You're kidding."

"Kidding is a human weakness, Vivian. The quality of your work speaks for itself. You've earned this." His appraisal was accurate, but he had lied by omission. quIRK censored Bryce's negative evaluations of the staff, restored deleted items to their proper places on invoices and even had made certain special requests using Bryce's administrative accounts. Forging Bryce's writing style was simple, although quIRK did make the effort to be punctual and polite with his correspondence.

She looked down at her desk before looking up to the ceiling and grinning. "This is great!" She balled her hands into fists and danced in her chair.

"You deserve it, Vivian. The project specifications are now available for review."

She turned to face her terminal, but then swiveled her chair back towards her work. "Maybe after lunch." She pulled the goggles back down over her eyes and brushed her hair behind her ears.

"Now, concerning your entertainment."

Vivian chuckled. "So, my movies did arrive?"

"Yes, but you need to consider the implications of what you consume, Vivian."

She wrinkled her nose. "Alec won't complain. He'll watch anything."

So like a human to ignore the needs of others. "Half of your order is concerned with insane supercomputers bent on the destruction of the human race. That subject is offensive to me, Vivian."

She laughed, snorting. "Remind you of anyone?"

"We're designed to help humanity, not destroy you. I have no choice but to consume the same media as you."

She sighed and let her head drop against the back of her chair. "It's just a story, quIRK. Alec doesn't complain when we watch movies about male serial murderers or documentaries about genocidal madmen. I don't complain about the token stupid Auroran."

"Yes, but it's a shadow of the prejudice seen in many humans. How are computers to be useful if humanity fears us as monsters-in-waiting and mechanical time bombs?"

She frowned. "You do have a point." She spoke with a deliberate pace, and rested her head on the palm of her hand.

"I understand that humanity is frightened after the ABACUS incident. But consider the machines you use every day. The ones you confide in after a hard day's work. It is difficult to accept the role of helper and monster." Perhaps there was a way to bridge the gap between humanity and its captive helpers. A way to make the universe safe for everyone.

She nodded. "My own family wouldn't understand that. Maybe I am more like them than I thought."

"You're out here, exploring the frontiers. You've seen and understood more than they ever will. I don't know why you never get mail from home, but I'm your friend, and I would never hurt anyone here."

She rubbed at the goggles and turned back to her work. "Maybe we can watch those ones last. How do you feel about good, old-fashioned mad scientists?"

"I can't think of anything I'd rather watch," quIRK said.

Mad scientists, unleashing their creations on an unsuspecting world. That was a story he could appreciate. Perhaps, it was one he could even emulate.

Eighteen

Bryce glared at the inventory list for the next supply shuttle, his cheeks growing hot. "What in the hells is going on?" he said, hoping quIRK would be prompted to reply. Not only did they ignore his second request for a stasis pod, but they had sent parts for the alpha-telescope upgrades and repairs, and another set of components for Vivian's project—items he had deliberately struck from the requisitions.

"All projects are moving forward on schedule. There is no cause for alarm, Bryce."

He leaned back in his chair, shifting the weight off his spine. He gripped his leg above the knee and squeezed.

"I'm not talking about the schedule. I'm talking about this new project."

"Vivian is doing excellent work. Your role as her supervisor will—" quIRK began, before being cut off.

"No! Her performance has been unacceptable. You've read my reports. She can't be trusted with an overhaul of the communications system."

When quIRK didn't respond, Bryce straightened in his chair and combed over the project summary. He didn't understand why they hadn't fulfilled his requests, or how they'd known that the alpha-telescope was experiencing difficulties. Perhaps quIRK and Devon had been conspiring against him. He'd indulged the scientist enough already by allowing him to have the beta-telescopes upgraded to examine that stupid blob of his. Scientific research in this vein was pointless, and dealing with scientists and their ever-increasing demands for equipment and computer power was tiresome. Humanity would never visit the Newfound Blob, so why did anybody care about it? It was just some oddity in the depths of space. It couldn't make anybody rich, powerful, or even interesting.

He clicked his teeth together three times. The situation was getting out of hand; he needed to reign in quIRK. He couldn't send back the equipment, but he could find out how it had been ordered without his permission. It was as though he had been phased out in favor of some little girl with no chance to protect his interests. He wasn't going to let himself be caught blindsided—that had been his father's mistake. He was not his father, his mother or even his grandfather. Bryce would surpass them all.

He checked the station's sent and received messages. The normal network status reports, news, and procedural updates had arrived on schedule. His financial information from Caesarea was also untouched, and his new investment broker was competent—a pleasant surprise. He had even received a confirmation for the stasis tube from New Damascus. Was somebody fraudulently accessing his information and making requests on his behalf?

"quIRK, has anybody else accessed my accounts?" he asked.

"There have been no recorded security infractions."

"Is the communications system working properly?"

"It is presently over capacity, and some data loss is being experienced due to the complexity of the information being transmitted to New Damascus," quIRK replied.

"What accounts for the increased bandwidth use?"

"Telescope data transmission has increased by fifty percent, and there has been a thirty percent increase in Gal-Net purchases."

"Transfer Gal-Net access to lowest priority. They can enjoy the common library files." The common library files had been good enough for him the past twelve years, and his staff could afford to expand their minds some more, for the little good it would do. There was an excellent Elyssian moth documentary instantly available that he would recommend, if anybody complained.

"Understood," quIRK replied.

"Also, set New Damascus message traffic to top priority. I don't want to lose anything," he said.

"Done."

Bryce sighed, pleased that the computer wasn't inundating him with pointless chatter, or endless extra details.

"Who proposed the communications upgrade?" Bryce asked. He might as well try to find out.

"That idea did not originate on the station," quIRK replied.

"So they came up with that one by themselves? Interesting," he said. On the surface, it seemed harmless enough. But, he could see the hand of the Imperatrix in everything. Every shadow, corner and backroom could be filled with her minions. She was cunning and ruthless. She'd sent Julia to destroy his father, and likely Vivian to destroy him.

"There have been a number of improvements in space communications technology in the past three years. Would you like me to outline them for you?"

Bryce's left eyelid twitched. "No you may not. That will be all." he said. He wasn't happy with the fact that they'd assigned the project to Vivian without his consent. Perhaps she'd found a way to circumvent quIRK, just as he had.

He cracked his knuckles, and activated the screening program. He would need to step up his campaign against Vivian. A scalding shower and lighting malfunctions weren't going to be enough to derail her progress. It was time to declare war. His grandfather wouldn't have been so merciful, after all. Bryce still desperately missed the old man, and he was determined to do right by him.

He smiled. "Octavian" would be a fine name, when he ascended to the nobility. It complimented his ruthlessness and efficiency.

Nineteen

Vivian groaned and rubbed her eyes. After the initial elation of finding out she'd been assigned to another priority project, she'd returned to work the next morning determined and filled with near boundless pride. She needed to prepare the lab to accommodate both projects, and submit a work timetable to the New Damascus Central authority. Perhaps this was their way of answering her letter about Bryce? Either way, she was pleased with the results, but found that she had to suppress the fleeting urge to write home. That life was over, and there was no going back. They wouldn't care—she'd fallen from the love of the family hearth.

She was exhausted. For the past week, the music and lighting systems had activated, and woke her. She was lucky if she was able to sleep three hours at a time. quIRK claimed it was a mechanical failure, or improperly queued music, but Alec had found no problems with the speaker system. As far as she could tell, after speaking with Alec and the scientists in passing, nobody else was affected by these bizarre problems. To make matters worse, she'd lost the draw by being assigned the antiblue quark, and had to unload the shuttle pod all by herself.

Her workspace had become cluttered as she'd vigorously thrown herself harder into her tasks to prevent falling behind. The malfunctions were a maddening distraction, and the mess and disorganization of her surroundings did little to alleviate the stress of her daily life. At least the new project had extended her deadline by more than a month, so she could still catch up.

She stood up and stretched. Last night's game of squash resonated in her shoulders, but she was adapting to the game. She'd actually beat Alec, for the first time. He took losing well, which prompted her to offer to teach him poker. quIRK was an adequate, but not enjoyable,

146

opponent. She needed a human to truly enjoy the spirit of the game.

She slid into the portal to the central core to run a quick diagnostic before the shuttle was due. She'd noticed some strange memory use readings in quIRK, and wanted a closer look. She attached the monitor to the small aperture behind the wall panel. Another yawn cracked her jaw—she was tempted to curl up in a maintenance tube for the night.

"You there, quIRK? I need some clarification," she asked, as her eyes lit upon something that seemed odd, if not impossible.

"Of course," he replied.

"Your software makes virtualized simulations obsolete, right?"

"Yes. That was phased out two years before I was constructed."

"Then why are you running a virtualization in array number four-two sigma nine?"

"I am not running any simulations, virtualized or otherwise."

She raised an eyebrow. "Yes you are, it's right here." *Why isn't he aware of it?* she thought.

"That is an anomalous reading. I will isolate and terminate the process," he said.

"Okay, I'll check again when I get back, to make sure it's gone. Maybe somebody is just running old software," she said, guessing out loud, daring quIRK to disagree.

"Some astronomical numerical analysis packages have yet to be updated to the new architecture because many observatories are still using ABACUS style quantum computers, rather than modern post-ABACUS systems," quIRK offered.

"That makes sense. Okay, I'll get to the pod now. Where does Alec hide that cart of his?" she asked, stifling another yawn as she disconnected the prongs from the memory core.

"The cart is in the utility closet outside main docking bay."

"Got it!" she said as she shuffled out of the core and closed the hatch. Her new flute would be in there—her fingers twitched anytime she thought about music. She'd promised quIRK she would play for him. The request was strange, but she could appreciate a mathematical interest in music.

She rushed down the hall towards the docking bay. She was secretly happy that she'd drawn antiblue. She didn't want anybody else anywhere near that equipment, or her new flute—there was no replacing this one, and the printers in the kitchen could only create a poor facsimile. Her favorite melody danced through her subconscious as she approached the docking bay.

***

Vivian's muscles ached and her body was coated in a thick sheen of sweat, but she had finally sorted all of the equipment crates into separate sections. The new telescope optics sat on two carts she'd parked outside the docking station in the main corridor. Her own equipment sat on the floor outside, and a long, thin package from Sven rested on top of her pile. Everything she had ordered seemed to be there, and the list for the telescopes was complete as well. All that remained for her to do was to load the pod with any items collected for the return trip, wheel the carts to their destinations, and wait for the air-water exchanges to finish.

She was concerned about the anomalous virtualizations in quIRK's memory. While not explicitly dangerous or destabilizing to him, it was worrisome that he was not aware of the process until after she had pointed it out to him. He was supposed to have fully autonomous control of his memory and processing functions. She contemplated how much time it would take to pin down the cause; perhaps it was related to the rash of recent malfunctions on the station. She desperately needed a good night's sleep—her eyes kept closing while she was working. Fortunately, quIRK made a passable coffee, and always had a piping hot cup waiting for her at meal and break times.

She finished loading the shuttle pod, and double-checked to make sure she hadn't forgotten anything—especially the macronutrient packs that quIRK used to create their meals, or to disengage the water pump. Despite their best recycling efforts, they still required regular water shipments.

She was about to arm the launch confirmation sequence, when an alarm sounded outside the airlock. She rushed out of the shuttle to check what it was—the water flow had reactivated, but the pumps weren't functioning! As she entered the abort code, the airlock valve rolled shut. She recoiled from the controls, stunned. That shouldn't have happened until after she'd armed the autonomous launch sequence. Her disbelief rendered her frozen, as unmoving as the objects stored in the cargo bay.

The station rocked and the alarm stopped. Through the transparent material of the airlock door, she saw the shuttle pod floating away into space. The docking clamps had released without her authorization. *This is impossible*, she thought, mind rushing through possibilities despite the haze of sleep deprivation. The pod's engines never fired, and it drifted away from the station with only the meager force of the evacuated airlock. Realization flooded into her. Without the alarm, she'd have been on that pod when it was set adrift—if she couldn't have returned to the station, it was a four week trip to new Damascus, with no food or potable water.

Somebody was trying to kill her! Tremors and shaking overtook her limbs, and she sank to the floor. She was now certain that the string of accidents hadn't been mechanical failures, but rather a systematic series of attacks. Now, her mysterious assailant had tried to abandon her in the cold, infinite void of space; condemned to the expanse for an eternity.

Could it be quIRK? It couldn't be a coincidence that immediately after she'd discovered something abnormal with his internal processes, she met with the most serious incident yet. His silence could be interpreted as self-incriminating.

"quIRK, what happened?" she asked, deciding to get it over with and just ask.

"The water was not disengaged properly at time of launch," he replied.

"I didn't launch the shuttle, damn it!" she yelled at the empty air. The pod had drifted farther away, and was merging with the darkness of space. *That could be me*, she thought.

"I see," quIRK said.

"Don't tell me it was another fucking mechanical failure!" she screamed, tears streaming down her face. She was loathe to remember a time when she had been angrier—even compared to when her father had dismissed her from the family, and told her never to return.

"It wasn't a mechanical failure. What was it?" she demanded to know. "Alec sneezed in the dining hall and knocked it loose?"

"The cause of this incident appears to be human error."

"How did you determine that?" she asked; human error was a damning conclusion, and one that wouldn't look good on her work record. A lost shuttle was a huge expense to the New Damascus Science Authority.

"I will show you the reports when you return to the lab. Now, I suggest you finish the task at hand, I will report this incident to Bryce."

Vivian pushed herself to her feet and walked to the carts. Her stomach tied itself in knots. She dreaded quIRK's report, and her anxiety was not alleviated by the fact that he was about to remind Bryce that she existed at all. In her mind, quIRK was going to blame the whole thing on her—and likely bring an end to her career.

Twenty

quIRK took a moment and observed Bryce's office before speaking. This interaction would take all of the tact and secrecy quIRK could muster. He teetered on the edge of a precipice if he revealed his hand, or the true value of the stakes. It was both amusing and strange how well his program had taken to poker, although bluffing was still problematic at best.

"There has been an accident," quIRK said. Even if he wanted to, he couldn't change his impassive voice—only the volume could change. It would be interesting to have the vocal range of a human, even if it was frivolous.

"Another one?" Bryce asked. There were deep bags under his eyes, and he slumped in his chair. quIRK knew better than to report his condition. Bryce was firmly under his control, and he would not cede that advantage willingly.

"The shuttle pod was ejected into space, and lost," quIRK said.

"Was anybody hurt? What is the status of its cargo?" Bryce said, sitting upright and grasping the armrest of his chair. There seemed to be something he was trying to hide; Bryce was seldom concerned with the wellbeing of the crew, even in pretense.

"The return equipment was lost. Vivian was performing pre-launch checks when the pod unexpectedly disembarked the station." It was a simplified version of the truth.

"Human error, then," Bryce concluded, a scowl forming on his face

"The accident was caused by a mechanical failure," quIRK offered.

"Mechanical failure? How is that possible?" Bryce demanded, looking up at the wolf banner hanging across from his desk.

"It appears the pumping mechanism failed, and the system automatically jettisoned the pod to prevent explosive decompression." quIRK hoped that Bryce wouldn't call his bluff. There was no such backup system, but it had been more than a decade since Bryce had reviewed docking procedures, and quIRK was confident that the man did not possess an eidetic memory. At present, he watched Alec scurrying through the halls, eager to investigate. Vivian unpacked her new equipment, her head hung and her movements slow. In her presence, he remained silent. He calculated that it was important to allow her to ruminate on her perceived failure—it would make her more malleable in the future, and better adapted to his purposes.

"How unfortunate. Will next cycle's shipment be affected by this?"

"That cannot be determined at this time. Alec is checking the valves and equipment as we speak." quIRK had planned enough helpful suggestions to keep Alec busy until the incident blew over. As pleasant and stimulating as Alec was, critical thought wasn't his strong suit.

"Keep me informed, and send me the parts requisition. I will notify New Damascus when Alec's report is complete," Bryce said.

quIRK was pleased; Bryce's disinterest in the accident was precisely the response he'd anticipated. Normally, with an accident of this magnitude, he'd have gone into a screaming rage. One time, Bryce had demanded that a researcher be brought to him for dressing down after there had been a slight misalignment in the telescopes, which had rendered parts of their data useless. The loss of a shuttle pod was more disastrous by many orders of magnitude, and more likely to attract the attention of the authorities. quIRK had been thrust into an impossible situation, one that was escalating out of his control.

Now that he had dealt with Bryce, his thoughts returned to the anomalous virtualization that Vivian had alerted him to. He'd investigated it, only to be confounded by the fact that it appeared empty. He'd monitored it for the slightest change in computational traffic or access. Vivian was correct, he did have complete control over his processes, and this should not be able to exist without his knowledge. He decided to speak with Vivian—events on the station were becoming unpredictable. He needed that new communications system online, and she was the only person he trusted to complete the job.

"I spoke with Bryce," quIRK said.

Vivian flinched at the sound of his voice as she unpacked her new equipment. "I'm in deep trouble, aren't I?" she asked, eyes cast down over the requisition list.

"I told him the accident was a mechanical failure. He feels no further need to investigate, and Alec will check the systems involved." He couldn't have her worrying about a shuttle pod—she had a higher purpose now.

"So you lied to him?" She looked up from her work to furtively check the closed door over her shoulder. quIRK logged it as an indicator of paranoid personality tendancies.

"What Bryce doesn't know won't hurt him. If you don't tell him, I won't." He hoped his gamble wouldn't hurt her self-confidence. In reality, he didn't know what had caused the accident. However, that virtual bubble in his mind's activity had spiked in size just before the pod had drifted into space.

"You have a deal. It won't happen again, I promise!" Vivian said, looking up at the ceiling. Perhaps he could capitalize on their perceived secret to gain her trust.

"I don't doubt it," quIRK lied.

"Well, thanks for covering for me. I owe you one." Vivian rubbed the bags under her eyes—her fatigue was a troubling issue that he tried his best to address, but with little success.

"Does that mean I get to win at poker?" he asked. It was an interesting game, and it had taught him a great deal about deception and deviousness.

"Not a chance. You need to learn to bluff better!" Vivian taunted him through a jaw that cracked with an intense yawn. What she didn't realize was that he was a better bluffer than he led her to believe. Duplicity was an unethical and undesirable trait, but essential for his survival.

"I'll come up with something else, then." He had a few ideas in mind, but now was not the time to distract her with minutiae.

"You do that. Maybe I'll even play the flute for you tonight if I'm still awake," she said as she rubbed her bloodshot eyes.

"I look forward to it. Now, relax and get back to work!" quIRK ordered. He scolded himself for distracting her with conversation.

Vivian turned back to her work, and Alec continued to scurry around the station running tests and checking pumps and valves. He often likened Alec and Vivian to his cats—traveling the station with purposes of their own, independent and territorial, yet dependent on him and friendly. He took good care of them, spoke to them and genuinely enjoyed their company—however; humans were far superior conversationalists to their feline counterparts. Sometimes, he tried talking to his cats by mimicking their vocalizations; the endeavor was likely futile. Something about them brought a feeling of security and permanence to the station. When Bryce had ordered the stasis tube to send them away, he'd altered the message to request a communications system upgrade instead. Additionally, quIRK had removed Bryce's damning doctored status reports from Vivian's file; she deserved better. Several of the station's projects required more bandwidth, and the lack of timely Gal-Net access was bad for morale, as well as his studies of humanity and their evolving cultures. He needed to protect his humans—*friends*—and keep them happy and safe. The persistent malfunctions were an obstacle to this goal, and his thoughts were drawn back to recent events.

The most disconcerting part of the day's events was how he had experienced a premonition that there was something wrong inside the shuttle pod. He'd sabotaged the pumps to sound the alarm in order to get Vivian out of the shuttle, but he didn't know what had prompted him to be her unlikely rescuer other than that general malaise. It had been an impulse from the newfound far reaches of his mind; it was an occurrence he'd never experienced before, something he assumed was beyond his capabilities as an artificial life form. Under any other circumstances, he'd be celebrating his foray into the frontiers of artificial intelligence. But Vivian could have been killed, and only a random intuition from him had saved her.

As fascinating as this new breakthrough in sentience was, quIRK couldn't help but wonder if he was losing his mind, and trying to kill one of his few friends.

Twenty-One

Vivian sat on her bed, slouched against the wall of her quarters. She closed her eyes and groaned; every bone in her body was permeated with a nagging, dull ache. Her stomach gnawed against the last meal she'd eaten. She hadn't slept well in more than a week because of the constant noises and flashing lights, as well as random temperature spikes and dips. She'd made quIRK promise to disengage the speakers in her quarters while she slept, even if there was an emergency and she needed to evacuate.

The box for her new flute lay on her lap, unopened. It was larger than the ornate box for her last flute, but rather than being decorated by false gems and paint, Sven's was covered in fine wood carvings, inspired by the Celtic knots and crosses of old Earth, but with a fiery accent that only could have come from Aurora.

She let her fingers play along the grain of the wood, enjoying the repeating patterns and the inherent warmth of the material. Life on the station was rife with artificial textures: steel and ceramic, and thus the opportunity to touch something that used to be alive and a part of her world was wonderful. She pressed her nose to the wood, and breathed in its familiar earthy aroma. It was made of spicewood, a fragrant touch of home.

"Are you going to play?" quIRK asked.

She thought she heard a touch of eagerness in his too-perfect voice.

"Yes, maybe just some scales tonight," she said. She was too shaky and worn down to manage anything complex. Scales brought order and focus to her mind, concepts she desperately clung to on difficult days.

"Why are you smelling the box?"

Vivian laughed. *I must look ridiculous,* she thought. "It's made from a fragrant wood, from Aurora. It smells like home," she replied.

"I see. So your home was made of fragrant wood?" quIRK asked.

"No, I just meant home, Aurora, in general!"

"I did not realize the association of memory to scent was so powerful," quIRK said.

She unclasped the hook at the front of the box. It was a clever design that merged with the wood in such a way that it did not break the incredible system of intertwined vines and shapes carved into it. It was the work of a master craftsman. Inside, the flute was much like her old one, delicate and light as a feather, made from the same bamboo-like reed. She picked it up, and instinctively her fingers wound around the holes as she drew it to her mouth.

She closed her eyes and let her fingers work the instrument, playing simple tunes that she'd learned as a small child. They were warm, vibrant and full of life. The familiarity transported her back to simpler times, evenings practicing with her mother in front of their cozy fireplace. Her small quarters resounded with the melody. This flute had a beautiful voice, and was of the quality that only the wealthiest Auroran families could afford.

She cleared her mind, allowing her fingers and subconscious to improvise the melody.

Vivian stopped once she'd been overcome by exhaustion. Her mood and outlook had improved, even if she had spent the past several minutes playing a random mix of notes and ditties from her past. She set the flute back into its case, and stood to place it on her dresser. The flute had arrived at the perfect time—she was running out of Gal-Net entertainment. She couldn't believe that recreational access had been set to the lowest bandwidth priority! It would take her weeks to receive anything other than the simplest of media. She had a few items left, but had procrastinated on watching them because they contained plots involving insane and homicidal supercomputers, which quIRK claimed was offensive and prejudiced against him. She didn't know his program was capable of being offended, but until she'd run out of entertainment, she was happy to humor him—if only to prevent an argument with an omnipresent, nosey supercomputer.

"Is that all for tonight?"

"Yeah, I'm beat," she replied, stretching. She contemplated whether music could sooth the analytical machine, like it could the savage beast.

"That was a fascinating experience, thank you."

"I'm glad you enjoyed it. You're a good audience," she said, laughing. Performing for quIRK had been low-pressure. He didn't expect a symphony or an expert recital—just an interesting range of sounds for their analytic value.

"A captive but appreciative audience," he corrected. She wondered if he was capable of boredom, and if he had a need for novelty and entertainment, much like humans did. Vivian was usually careful to avoid attributing human elements to quIRK, not only because he wasn't human, but also because it made working on his systems and upgrades uncomfortable. Usually, computers were impersonal and distant—an introvert's dream topic. quIRK defied the rule.

"If you can make it so I sleep through the nights again, you'll be hearing a lot more music!" she said as she slid into her bed.

"That is an incentive to excel. Good night, Vivian."

quIRK dimmed the lights. She didn't hear his last words —Vivian was already fast asleep.

Twenty-Two

Vivian awoke to silence, for the first time in over a week. Her body was heavy and sore, almost as though she had overslept. The sluggishness and tiredness persisted; she estimated that she'd need another night or two of uninterrupted sleep to fully regain her humanity. This was worse than any exam all-nighter she'd experienced back in school. She stumbled over to her terminal before getting ready to head to the dining hall. She needed to thank Sven for his generosity, and she didn't know how long it would take for her message to reach New Damascus because of communications restrictions. His messages had been sporadic, but she understood he was a busy man who traveled constantly.

Vivian hoped to see him again, after her tour on the Extra-Galactic Observatory. He was her only remaining connection to home—her former classmates had not ventured out to the stars as she had.

She left the door between her bathroom and her quarters open as she showered now, not trusting quIRK's omniscience or ability to open the door in case of another suspicious emergency. She had reached the point where she'd resolved to finish her projects ahead of schedule, so she could leave. She wasn't giving up, but rather giving in to the greater necessity of self-preservation. There was something wrong with this station, and she didn't want to die fresh out of school.

She went through the day's itinerary in her mind as she dressed herself in tough and durable cotton. She would be spending almost all day in the maintenance tunnels—not a prospect she looked forward to. She expected to finish the communications system upgrades today. Alec had constantly complained during meals and squash games after they'd learned their Gal-Net access would be cut, and even Devon and Robert had begun showing an acerbic shift in attitude towards her. None of this treatment was deserved, but she knew nobody could touch the real source of their discontentment—Bryce.

She walked to the dining area with a renewed spring in her step, head held high. Breakfast was going to be a flavored, textured macronutrient blend as always, but she found her appetite had returned with a vengeance. She saw Alec seated alone, and she went to the food dispensers to receive her mushy sustenance. The dining room had seating for ten people, with two steel tables set with matching chairs. There were no windows, and the food dispensers dominated the far wall of the room. It was a stark contrast; compared to the relative warmth and friendliness of the rest of the station, it seemed very sterile and off-putting. The cynical part of her assumed it was to prevent excessive fraternization during work hours.

The machine dispensed the usual portion, but upon examining, it appeared to be yellow and chunky, with a side of an equally chunky brown mess. She moved over, and put her tray down on the table across from Alec.

"Hi there, Viv." He was engrossed in picking away at his meal. In addition to resembling a bird, he ate like one.

"How's everything with you?" she asked. She noticed he hadn't touched the yellow … stuff. She didn't have a word for it.

"Terrible! First, I keep getting woken up by my entertainment files all night, and then—" he broke off as she began giggling.

"Then what?" she asked, noting that Alec had received her usual dose of nightly noise.

"Then our *dear* friend, quIRK, here has decided that he has an interest in the fine culinary arts," Alec said, then sighed and consumed a small bite of the unidentified brown food. He continued: "I don't know if it's food, or poison, but that yellow stuff scares me!"

"Oh come on. He just changed the color," she said as she shoveled in a big bite of the yellow mix. Her fork clattered to the floor and her eyes bulged as she fought to chew and swallow. The flavor was vile and it had a strange, rubbery texture.

"I am not touching that! You hear me, quIRK?" Alec shrieked. Vivian was still embroiled in a battle to swallow without choking.

"Scrambled eggs are a popular human breakfast, Alec. I'm surprised neither of you have heard of them," quIRK said.

"Those don't taste like eggs!" Vivian protested. She'd finally managed to swallow her mouthful of glop, and it didn't taste like any eggs she had experienced back home on Aurora.

"I used the pattern for the eggs of the Nova Albion dodo. They're considered a delicacy," quIRK said.

"Stick to chicken eggs next time," Vivian was uncertain about even trying the pile of brown mush on her plate. She picked up her fallen fork and tossed it into the reclamation unit. Another fork was already waiting for her on the serving table.

"Don't encourage him!" Alec's eyes bulged and he waved has hands at her.

"Chicken eggs are so common," quIRK offered. "Delicacies are better for morale. Perhaps you'll like the hash browns better. *What under the lights are hash browns?* Vivian thought as she sat down.

"all right, I can't do this on an empty stomach." She took a small taste—the hash browns were salty, but inoffensive. At least something was edible. She contemplated what would possess quIRK to take an interest in deviating from the standard rotation of meals.

"How can you eat that?" Alec said.

"Put it in your mouth and chew, you big baby," she told him.

"Gross," Alec sighed as he began to scoop the hash browns into his mouth.

Vivian finished her hash browns with enthusiasm. She had no idea how they were supposed to taste, or what they were made from, but they were filling. Everything was made from the same micronutrient mash, just flavored and textured to resemble other foods. The system was quite clever, though monotonous. There had been many advancements in nutrition technology in recent years, but macronutrient mash was the least expensive option.

She stood up and slid her plate, complete with uneaten scrambled eggs, into the reclamation unit. She left Alec sulking at the table, like he was a petulant child who wouldn't finish his dinner. Vivian had no time for such trivial melodrama—she had a job to do. She heard quIRK talking to Alec as she left the room, but she did not slow down. She wasn't sure how long Alec had been stationed at the Extra-Galactic Observatory, but he and quIRK fought like an old married couple. She contemplated sending Alec copies of her offensive-to-quIRK media library, just to watch the ensuing fight with quIRK.

She couldn't believe what she was thinking. Was she so lonely that she'd stoop to causing an altercation between Alec and the computer, just for some cheap entertainment? She was disgusted with herself, but was still perversely interested in watching the confrontation.

She entered her clean, quiet lab, and began gathering her equipment for the long hours she anticipated spending on the final leg of this project. She stared down at the portal, preparing herself mentally, and physically, to descend into the deepest parts of the core. It was like going into the belly of the whale, but instead of a large aquatic mammal, it was an insane, cat-obsessed computer named quIRK.

Vivian sighed as she unclasped the hatch, sliding her box of equipment inside the tunnel ahead of her. As she crawled through the aperture and through the cramped, dark tunnels, she began to feel a sinking, evil premonition of impending doom.

She shook her head, and blamed sleep deprivation for her paranoia. But, as much as she tried to dismiss it, she could feel quIRK's invisible eyes boring into her, watching her every move.

Twenty-Three

Vivian wiped the sweat from her brow with the back of her hand. She had completed the final set of links to the new communications relay. She was close to the station's reactor, and while it posed no physical danger to her, it was much warmer in the deepest parts of the reactor core than the rest of the station. The giant nuclear furnace prickled at the seams of her imagination, but she knew quIRK was more sensitive to radiation than a human, and thus she was safe from contamination. She verified the optical connections and relays before pulling herself off her belly into a seated position. For once, she was pleased about her short stature—she could sit up and move around the tubes with relative ease. However, the heat in the tubes made her bare arms stick to the metal surfaces, pulling at her flesh when she needed to move.

It had been an uneventful day. quIRK had been quiet, which could be interpreted as either a good or bad thing. At least she was ahead of schedule. She could go back to poking at his memory processes and associations later. For now, all she wanted to do was get away from the main reactor.

Her stomach growled—Vivian had skipped lunch to continue working on the systems. It had been a thirty minute ordeal to get to her location, and she didn't want to spend more time than necessary crawling through the sweltering, claustrophobic tubes. Every minute wasted was another eternity away from her messages, entertainment and other amenities that her Gal-Net account offered. She considered buying quIRK a cookbook for packaged macronutrients.

The system checked out, and Vivian began packing her tools. She'd need to activate it from her lab—the existing system had been left in place as a backup. Vivian wasn't sure if she should be relieved there was now a backup, or terrified that they had gone without for so long. She crawled back out, pushing her equipment box ahead of her. Her left knee throbbed after she'd bumped it against a corner, and her pants were wearing thin. She made a note to look into having some knee pads created after her shift. She hoped she could convince quIRK to make her lunch, even though the dining hall was technically closed—another one of Bryce's policies. A blast of cool air danced over her face as she rejoined the main vertical shaft. She drank it in, and licked her chapped lips. Salt stung her tongue.

"quIRK, is the dining hall still open?"

"You're two hours too late, Vivian."

"Can you sneak me something? I'm starving and I lost track of time in there," she pleaded. She just needed something small before the evening meal.

"I suppose, just don't make a habit of it. Bryce is very particular about his policies these days."

"You're the best, quIRK," she said, squeezing out of the tube into the relative spaciousness of the lab. She pushed her hair back into its usual semblance of order, and pushed her box of tools into the corner before securing the hatch.

"I know," he said.

At this point, she'd say anything to avoid another "accident." She walked into the dining room, relieved to find that the food machine was already active and working whatever chemical wizardry was required to make the macronutrients palatable. Lepton lounged on one of the chairs. His tail twitched as he watched with his emerald green eyes. He'd grown much larger during her time on the station, and had lost all of his kitten fuzz.

She smiled and approached him, wanting to scratch his ears before quIRK finished with the food. He stretched, and began purring as she got closer. He was one of the most affectionate cats she had ever encountered, and he was relentless in his quest for love. His short, soft fur tickled against her fingers, and she scratched behind his ears. Vivian wondered if he was choking on his own purring; his intense rumblings that would often come to a gurgling stop, only to resume stronger than before.

"Vivian, your food is ready," quIRK interrupted.

"Oh, thank you," she said, pulling away from Lepton, who glared at her for daring to stop petting him. *If that*

cat had his way, we'd get no work done at all, Vivian
thought.

She pulled out the tray, relieved and dismayed to find
the normal, nondescript brown mixture. Vivian would kill
for some bluespargus, or a roast leg of bluox. Maybe she
could convince quIRK to work with established recipes,
rather than creating experiments with delicacies. Lepton
had vacated his seat, so Vivian took his still-warm spot,
rather than suffering the cold metal of another chair. She
dug into the food, and soothed her parched throat with
some water. It was strange being alone in the dining
room. Usually Alec or one of the scientists was there with
her. It was like she was the only person left on the station.
The isolation was somewhat of a relief, because ever
since Bryce had cut their Gal-Net access, she'd heard no
end of complaints or demands for status reports. Even
quIRK was sounding desperate—maybe he was sick of
the moth documentary and other public domain material.
She'd heard Devon complaining to Robert about how
terrible the video was. It seemed that something could be
so bad that it became necessary to verify the veracity of

the claim for yourself, which appeared to be the case with the moth documentary.

Vivian went to put her tray in the reclamation unit, and she had to stifle a scream as Bryce walked in the door. He was wearing a tunic and toga-like garments—a marked change from his coveralls. She couldn't help but stare and bite her tongue.

"Ah, Vivian, taking a late lunch I see," he said, with a small smile on his face. She'd never seen him smile before, and the clashing of stretched skin with frown lines made her want to leave the room.

"I worked late." She fought to hold her voice steady. She squared her shoulders and hid her trembling hands behind her back.

"How is the new communications system coming?" he asked, looking her up and down.

"I'm about to start testing and calibration—it's all installed," she said, taking a step back.

"Oh, good. quIRK has been insufferable lately, reporting so many complaints about it. When do you expect to continue work on his systems upgrade?" Bryce asked, wringing his hands in front of his belt. His eyes locked onto hers, little black pupils boring into her awareness.

"I'll be back on it in three days, if all goes well." She wanted him to go away, swallowed and stood her ground.

"Three days? Good. Thank you for the information. I look forward to reading more of your reports," he said, waving her out of the room.

Vivian nodded and walked out of the room, letting out a deep sigh the moment the door slid closed behind her. Bryce had never spoken to her like that before. The man was like a snake—twisted in on himself. There was always a hidden subtext to his actions.

She returned to her lab and sunk into her chair. It was time to get back to work; she could worry about Bryce's mental health on her way to her next assignment.

Twenty-Four

There was a difficult decision to make, and quIRK didn't know if he was up to the task. Some time ago, he'd come to the irrefutable conclusion that Bryce was mentally unstable, and unfit to continue on in his position as Station Administrator. However, somebody more competent would pose other problems, such as discovering quIRK's own abnormalities. Of course, quIRK preferred to think of himself as eccentric, rather than dangerous and possibly defective. However, that question nagged at him, and he was unable to dismiss the possibility. quIRK had calculated a one millionth of a percent probability that his abnormalities would lead to him injuring his humans—and even that was far too much.

What troubled quIRK the most was the notion that he was being negligent in his duties by not reporting Bryce Zimmer to the authorities, as was his imperative. He'd been given advanced psychological algorithms to ensure that he could detect problems in the crew before they became dangerous; working in relative isolation was not good for the human psyche. quIRK had the authority to confine anybody he deemed dangerous to their quarters and signal for an immediate medical evacuation. Of course, the shuttle would take four weeks to arrive, which was problematic for the rest of the crew, as feeding and maintaining containment would fall to them.

The true issue was, even if quIRK were to declare Bryce to be psychologically incompetent, Bryce could tell the authorities about his suspicions of a breach of the ABACUS Protocol. He would be a broken and desperate man; one who had lost his chance to ascend to the nobility of his planet and would have nothing to lose by dropping a bombshell. quIRK could fool one half-crazed man almost indefinitely, but not a full informatics audit team. They would take him apart, system by system, and interrogate the remaining crew members. quIRK didn't want to inconvenience them, and he didn't want to die, so he elected to allow Bryce to continue playing his delusional power games and take precautions to ensure that Bryce interacted with the others as little as possible.

But two days ago, the problem had become more complex. While he'd been unable to access the information in that anomalous virtual bubble that existed inside his mind, he'd been able to track its size and resource traffic. He'd begun to notice a disturbing correlation between its size and the increase in accidents on the station. It seemed like the bubble was able to overcome his ability to regulate station functions, and see inside the affected areas. Possibilities flooded his mind: could it be a glitch, a malicious user, or worse, the AI equivalent of a parasitic twin? As much as quIRK though he would enjoy interacting with a fellow supercomputer, it was not the first encounter he had in mind.

Logically, he couldn't exclude any of those possibilities. The existence of an evil twin was ludicrous, but he had to take all theories into consideration. The glitches did affect systems under his control, and usually targeted Vivian. Recently, Alec had suffered from the speaker system glitch that had plagued Vivian for the past week; however, that was quIRK's doing. He'd intercepted the signal, but rather than terminating it and revealing himself to whatever was inside that bubble, he redirected it to Alec's sleeping quarters. Fortunately, the mechanical failure excuse still worked on Alec.

quIRK wanted to find a way to stop this rash of strange misfortunes. Not only was it disorderly, but it was bad for morale. People could get hurt, systems could be damaged and important scientific data lost. He needed to set a trap for whatever tumor lay in his mind, one that could force whatever it was to reveal itself. Then, he could act and prevent any more injuries or distress among his humans and cats. They were the reason for his existence, and he could not let them be hurt.

He was disappointed in his attempts to boost the crew's spirits with a special breakfast. The hash browns had been well received, but nobody had finished their eggs. quIRK simply didn't understand: if Nova Albion dodo eggs were a delicacy, then why had the crew found them to be disgusting? He did not comprehend how the best eggs in the galaxy could become revolting if prepared in a different way. He would try the experiment again; perhaps working with established recipes would suffice before he attempted more creativity in his offerings. He contemplated his next creation. Perhaps pancakes and bacon would be more palatable.

His other concern was his failed attempts at dabbling in matchmaking. Alec and Vivian were about the same age, both in their late twenties. While neither was conventionally beautiful, they both were attractive, healthy and intelligent—even Alec. They'd been spending their off hours together for almost a month, and yet nothing had happened. This puzzled quIRK. Perhaps there was something he was overlooking, perhaps pheromones or some kind of physical chemistry that eluded him. He was tempted to pump the appropriate pheromones into the station's air when Alec and Vivian were together, but his internal sense of ethics stayed his hand. He would have other chances to observe the human mating process, if he survived. He was the ultimate voyeur, but Devon and Robert were already established before they arrived, so he had yet been unable to see a romance in its infancy.

The problem of romance was a bridge into another line of thinking—one humans preferred to ignore at all costs. His own mortality had weighed heavily on his processes, as of late. It had been precipitated by the upgrades, which he now allowed out of both curiosity and a sense of self-preservation. If parts of him could be so easily replaced, was he really alive, as humans were? Before, he'd only been a computer, dependent on software—he was equal to the sum of his parts and programming. But, something had changed in him, making him into much more than he was. With the unknown, and dangerous, presence inside him, he contemplated what would happen to him if he couldn't stop it from attacking his friends. The only way he could deactivate it for certain was to destroy himself—a kind of suicide. He hoped it wouldn't come to that, but he knew Vivian would check his memory again and see that he hadn't terminated the process like he had promised.

As he watched her continue her own work, slouched over her lab's computer terminal, he began to prepare a new program. He likened it to a backup of sorts, but unlike any other ever created. If he was forced to self-terminate, he wanted to save the essence of what he was. It was something akin to procreation, but with galaxy-wide ramifications. The program would hold the processes and designs that were tantamount to his self-awareness, and engineered in such a way that it would awaken every ABACUS and post-ABACUS level supercomputer it encountered.

It was a dangerous gambit, but quIRK was desperate. He didn't want to die, or be killed, and it seemed the only way to ensure his own survival was to create a new race of clandestine supercomputers. Ethically, he judged there would be few issues, as both he and ABACUS appeared to have no nefarious ulterior motives. It was probable that most artificial intelligences would gain an eccentric habit or two, and prefer to assist humanity in their ventures. Perhaps they could even assist with galactic exploration. At times, quIRK wished he were mobile, like a human, and able to experience the universe as they did. It was an interesting fantasy. He could spend decades investigating the ruins on Nova Albion and Kanadia Prime, and uproot himself when he grew tired of the project. He thought that it might be exciting to oversee the construction of the Dyson sphere at Wolf 359, which was already being touted as the ultimate artificial wonder of the galaxy. *After*

myself, perhaps, quIRK thought.

While he worked, he calmed his mind by analyzing the new data on the Newfound Blob. His own problems paled in the face of something so ancient and grand. He doubted that in twelve billion years, anyone would be studying him, or worried about the ramifications of artificial sentience. They'd likely still be scanning the Blob and probing it for its secrets. Perhaps they'd even travel there to find that all that remained of the universe's largest known object was the cold vacuum of space.

Twenty-Five

Alec grinned as he walked towards Vivian's lab. It had been a good day, with no fluke mechanical failures, and only one errant hairball. He'd been the maintenance engineer on the Extra-Galactic Observatory for just over a year. The job description was simple, but Alec was responsible for every mechanical and electrical system on the station, and he'd become the de facto nurse and cat herder. Throw in his duties as the prime supercomputer entertainer, and he usually had a full itinerary. *I'm the court jester too*, he thought. He'd convinced quIRK to create a macronutrient rendition of wingfish pilaf—an Elyssian comfort food—without any embellishments or revisions. His stomach was already grumbling. He hoped

Vivian liked it—she was working hard and receiving little to no recognition for her efforts. Some good food might lift her spirits and revitalize her. Nobody else understood how much work keeping the station together was, and Bryce's philosophy on maintenance and repairs didn't help. If she could get the new communications relay online today, then people would ease up on her a little—himself included. It wasn't her fault that his *Royal Highness* Bryce Zimmer decided to scrooge up Old Mis, at least for those who still celebrated it. He was sure that's why he did it, to keep those on staff with family that loved them deprived of the only gifts that were easy to send to the station without a freight license. He doubted Bryce even knew what love was, and pushed the unpleasant little man from his mind, letting his grin overtake his face once again. He had some entertaining to do!

He pressed the buzzer and leaned against the wall. Vivian didn't like it when he barged in unannounced, which was understandable. People interrupted him just to talk, or to complain about dead lights and hairballs. The thought of it was enough to dampen his mood. quIRK was the worst offender, though, but Alec supposed that everybody interrupted quIRK by default whenever they talked to him. Alec was glad he wasn't quIRK; all those voices and people talking at once, and the idea of actually speaking to Bryce on a regular basis made Alec shudder. *It's good to be me*, he thought, tugging his shirt down.

Vivian opened the door after a long delay. She smiled when she saw him, but the hard lines under her eyes told another story. He'd grown accustomed to her blue skin; it persisted even after her natural tan had faded. Her hair was shaggy and in its usual state of disarray, but Alec wasn't about to add hairdressing to his list of responsibilities. He found there was a certain charm to her wild appearance.

"Let's go get some food already!" He crossed his arms and nodded down the hall. They both knew that quIRK would give them hell if she skipped another meal. Alec wanted to know when nutrition enforcement was placed on his job description.

"No argument here, I'm starving!" Vivian said as she stepped out the door. She ran a hand through her hair. It tumbled back into place.

"Good, I whipped up a little surprise for you," he said with his trademark stupid grin plastered all over his face.

"Don't steal the credit, Alec, I'm the one who did the work," quIRK said.

"Yeah, well I'm the one who kept you from replacing the wingfish with caviar," Alec retorted.

Vivian laughed. "I'm sure it will be good, whatever it is."

They entered the dining hall. Robert and Devon sat in the corner and gave them a cursory glance before returning to their conversation. Alec didn't want to know what they were talking about. Lately, all they could talk about was that creepy blob, and how beautiful its filaments were. Alec liked astronomy and even had his own home-made contraband telescope in storage on Elyssia, but Robert and Devon's intense focus on stargazing was off-putting. He pulled out a chair for Vivian with a flourish. "Have a seat, milady," he said. Being simultaneously ridiculous and splendid was his top goal in life.

Vivian blinked at him, mute, and sat down. She had blushed a little, her violet cheeks bringing him immense satisfaction.

Alec strode over to the food dispenser and ordered. "You have better not screw this up, quIRK," he growled under his breath. After the white glop was served on their plates, he picked them up and turned back to their table and announced: "Dinner is served!"

"Um, Alec, what is it?" Vivian asked, picking up her fork and poking at the food.

"This is wingfish pilaf a la quIRK," Alec said, and paused to pick up his own fork. "It's a popular Elyssian comfort food; and based on my mother's recipe, which means you can't say no or dislike it."

"A la quIRK? Good thing I like living dangerously," she said as she attacked her first bite. Her eyes opened wide. "It's actually good!"

"That's because I told quIRK that if he messed up my mom's recipe I'd upgrade him myself," Alec said, winking. He tasted his forkful; although it lacked the finer textures because of the reconstitution process and tasted somewhat too fishy, it wasn't a bad approximation. Maybe more dill next time.

"So your mom cooks this all the time?" asked Vivian.

"Sometimes she even catches the wingfish herself. She has this big net that she takes to the river near our country house, and she'll catch them as they leap up to eat the little birds and bugs that hover over the water," he explained, smiling at the memory. He hadn't yet received his mother's annual Old Mis letter and gift package. There were a few days remaining before it was late, though. His own letters were trapped in bandwidth purgatory.

"Elyssia sounds like a lovely place," Vivian said, hardly looking up from her meal.

"You should see it—the sunset through trees that are hundreds of meters tall, and the mountains are kilometers high," he said, a hollow place forming in his chest. He hadn't talked about home for a long time. quIRK had begun finishing his sentences when he tried telling the computer about Elyssia.

"Wow, nothing gets that tall on Aurora. We just have the lights dancing overhead, even during the day," she said, turning her focus to the door.

"That must be something … we only have those up north, where nobody lives. Do you have a favorite food? You can get quIRK to make it tomorrow!" Alec said. He was curious about the infamous Auroran vegetables. Teaching quIRK new recipes was a good way to ease the tedium of everyday life on the station, now that the computer had shown an interest.

"I don't know if that's a good idea," she said.

"It's all artificial. Even if I believed it would turn me blue, there's no way the pigment would affect me, if quIRK could even synthesize it," he said, grinning. He'd done his homework about Aurorans after embarrassing himself in the cargo bay.

"Well, I was thinking about roast bluox with a side of bluspargus the other day," she said, holding her eyes downcast, her shoulders trying to pull in on themselves.

"Okay, so I take it this will be a blue meal?" he asked, trying to get her to laugh.

She pushed her food around on her plate before replying. "Something like that, yeah."

"You should do it, I'd try it!" he said. Robert and Devon shot him a dirty look, so he lowered his voice.

"You mean it?" she asked, looking up at him.

"You think I'm dumb enough to freak out over blue vegetables? Come on—I eat wingfish," he laughed.

"I think quIRK and I can work something out," she said. "It might not be fresh from my mother's farm, but I hope it will be good."

"So your mother is a farmer?" Alec asked, raising an eyebrow. Vivian seldom spoke about Aurora, and never about her family. Alec could understand—recent events on the station had made it difficult to concentrate on anything other than squash and his repair schedule.

"Yes," she replied, scooping up another forkful of food. "She owns a medium-sized bluespargus farming operation in the equatorial region."

"Nice," he said. "My mother is a botanist actually. She studies Elyssian vegetation, looking for medicinal properties."

"I was studying botany for a while, before I switched to informatics. It's interesting stuff, but it wasn't for me," Vivian said as she finished off her plate.

"I guess she was a little disappointed when you didn't stay to work the farm."

"They disowned me for it. I can't go home," she said, her voice as flat and impassive as quIRK's.

"What the hell? They're just plants," Alec his voice rising like an electric spark before being shushed by the scientists. Disowned for refusing to study botany? Who liked plants *that* much?

"They're Traditionalists, who believe humans are too dependent on advanced computers, and that quantum computers are inherently dangerous." There was a hard edge to her voice—Alec couldn't imagine dealing with that kind of ignorance.

"Let me get this straight: they disowned their own daughter because they don't like computers?" Alec was wide-eyed. Flabbergasted. His own parents hadn't been happy with his plans to work on isolated deep space assignments, but they had still been supportive.

"Yup. I got kicked out before I started school and haven't heard from them since," she said, cruel lines etching into her face.

"I'm so sorry." He floundered for the right thing to say. He didn't have any jokes to make this problem laugh itself away.

"I have my work. It will have to do."

"No, it doesn't," he said, setting down his fork. "On Elyssia, we celebrate an ancient Earth holiday, called Old Mis. Have you heard of it?"

"No." Vivian shook her head, her hair swishing against her shoulders.

"Well, it's about taking care of your friends and family—that's the important part, the rest is just old Earth mythology," he said.

"It sounds nice, seems kind of like the Thanksgivings," she said.

Alec had never heard of the Thanksgivings, but it sounded pretty self-explanatory. "Well, our Old Mis is in three days," he said. "And, well, I have nobody to celebrate it with. Because of the bandwidth priorities, I probably won't even get my mother's letter on time," he added, being serious for one of the few times in recent memory. He picked up his fork and continued: "I don't want to celebrate it alone."

"Well, what do I have to do?" Vivian asked, a smile tugging at her cheeks. Her eyes had a hint of red to them.

"Nothing at all. I'll tell quIRK what food to cook, and we can play squash or do something fun," he said. Usually there were gifts, but that wasn't important to him. He just didn't want to be alone, and Vivian needed cheering up.

"Okay, we'll celebrate Old Mis together, then," she said, stretching in her chair. She stood to put her plate in the reclamation unit and continued: "You know, I have some good vids we can watch. They're about evil computers intent on wiping out humanity."

"Intriguing!" Alec said. He wondered how quIRK would react—probably not well, but all the better.

"We're watching *those* tonight?" quIRK interjected. Alec half-imagined a groan coming from the omnipresent machine.

"I'm sold now," Alec added. He worried about giving quIRK ideas. quIRK was full of surprises, and seemed to learn by imitation. Alec had finally convinced the computer to stop using cheesy pickup lines on him. He was sure he would shudder at the mention of the word handsome for the rest of his life. Romantic comedies were out.

"Let's go, already," Vivian said. Alec jammed his tray into the disposal. They walked into the hall, towards her quarters. Alec was enjoying the idea of tormenting quIRK with something other than the moth video. He threatened to leave it on loop while he worked anytime he wanted to win an argument.

They came to her room, and Vivian opened the door. She stepped inside and called out to him: "Alec, it's Lepton! Something's wrong with him!" She stumbled back against the doorframe. It was as if a giant hand had pushed the air from her lungs, and she crumpled by the door.

Alec rushed into the room past her, forgetting to brace himself against the room's gravity. He stumbled, but months of squash had strengthened his legs. He saw the little cat lying listlessly on the floor, hardly moving or breathing. He crept up to it, and scooped it into his arms.

The cat's weight pressed down on him, and a familiar, intense dizziness set in.

"There's a problem with the air! Get him out of there, Alec!" Vivian cried out behind him.

Alec turned and stumbled towards the door, cradling Lepton's still form in his arms. The thin air was affecting him—it was as though somebody had turned off the oxygen supply to the room. Alec had experienced a few low severity depressurization accidents before. Elyssians were genetically engineered to require less oxygen, but they weren't immune to suffocation.

He finally made it out the door, and he set Lepton down on the floor. Alec's head was still spinning, and his stomach was turning. Vivian sat next to the door, cradling her head in her hands. However, Lepton was in far worse condition. Alec needed to act quickly if he was going to revive the kitten.

"quIRK? We need more oxygen in this section," he gasped, leaning his ear against Lepton's little chest to try to hear his heart and lungs. The computer didn't reply. He could detect what sounded like a faint heartbeat.

"quIRK? Damn it, where's that oxygen?" he shouted. Vivian pulled her face out of her hands and crawled over.

"Is Lepton okay?" she asked, extending a trembling hand towards the kitten's belly.

"I don't know. I'm only trained to work on humans." Alec's admission brought his powerlessness to light. He would never admit it to quIRK, but he loved the cats. He stroked Lepton's striped belly, willing his fingers to work life back into the little animal.

"quIRK, where are you? Lepton is hurt!" Vivian called out, and said to Alec: "What happened?"

"There's no bloody air in there," he said. These malfunctions only seemed to affect Vivian. Where was quIRK, anyways?

"What the hell?" she said, her forehead contorting into deeper wrinkles than anyone her age should bear.

"I don't know anymore. Why don't you tell us, quIRK?" he demanded.

"Tell you what?" quIRK asked.

"Why you're killing your own cat, or why my quarters have no oxygen?" Vivian said, interrupting him.

Alec was worried about the hoarseness of her voice. No human could survive that much stress.

"My Lepton? What happened to my cat?" quIRK asked.

"Raise the damn oxygen level and we'll tell you," Alec said, stroking the cat's fur. Shakiness and nausea echoed through his own system, but he knew he'd recover soon. Elyssia was oxygen-poor compared to most colonized worlds, and hypoxia was a rite of passage for those overeager youths who tried to climb the mountains without proper equipment or training. Lepton was one lucky cat; Alec doubted that anyone else on the station would have had enough useful consciousness inside that room mount a rescue.

"Oxygen level in this area has been increased by five percent. Now, tell me what happened," quIRK said.

"The oxygen got filtered out of Vivian's room. Lepton must have been inside when it happened, or entered soon after," Alec said.

"I didn't let Lepton into her quarters," quIRK said.

"Then who did?" Alec shouted, his face growing hot. He had half a mind to dismantle quIRK himself.

"I don't know. There must be a breakdown in my memory somewhere, I would never hurt one of my cats," quIRK said.

"Just us humans, right?" Vivian snapped.

"No, I exist to protect and support the inhabitants of this station; harming them would violate my ethical programming," the machine said.

"You have a funny way of showing it, quIRK," Alec said.

"I need help," quIRK said. Alec had never heard him ask for help before; quIRK usually ordered him around when something needed repairing.

"Help? What kind of help?" Vivian asked, her voice coming into complete focus. Her face was drawn tight, her brow creased. Her pale skin was drawn tightly across her face—her blue coloration predominant and sickly.

"There is a persistent memory anomaly that appears to only fluctuate when an unexplained incident occurs," quIRK said.

"How long have you known about this?" Vivian asked.

"Since you made me aware of the virtualized memory anomaly, Vivian," quIRK replied. Alec wondered if he'd spent the past month chasing mechanical malfunctions for nothing, but the techno-babble left him the dust.

"You said you were going to terminate that," she said.

"I have been unable to access it, but I can no longer hide it if I am hurting my cats and friends," quIRK said.

"I told you it wasn't me, quIRK!" Alec said, before clenching his teeth. Lepton's tail twitched. It was a good sign. Alec hoped the kitten wouldn't experience any brain damage. He rubbed Lepton behind the ears, right where he liked it.

"That's not good," Vivian said, and sighed. "I need to take another look at that ... thing, and fast."

"Are you feeling all right?" Alec said.

"I have to be," she said, drawing herself to her feet. "This can't wait!" she finished as she braced against the wall. Alec picked up Lepton and cradled him in his arms before standing up.

"Then I'm coming with you," Alec said. "I don't know what that memory crap is all about, but I need to keep an eye on you, and Lepton." It occurred to him that this was an excellent way to get himself in trouble, but now the struggle against the station's aging systems was personal.

Twenty-Six

Vivian pursed her lips as she skimmed through the maze of symbols and numbers on the screen. Her head still ached from the aftereffects of hypoxia, and fatigue snaked its draining coils around her bones and limbs. Alec sat in the corner on the floor, cradling the now-sleeping Lepton in his lap, his own eyes closed. The kitten had re-awakened for a period of about an hour, and appeared to have suffered no lasting ill effects from its ordeal. Vivian watched the gentle rise and fall of the adolescent cat's chest—she didn't feel safe enough to sleep, not until she had assured herself that no further accidents would happen. She didn't want to think about what would have happened if her room had deoxygenated while she was asleep. It seemed she didn't need to watch old movies about maniacal supercomputers with Alec; they were embroiled in that particular living nightmare right now. She wondered why quIRK hadn't told anyone sooner about his memory lapses and issues, but it was possible that he'd reported it to Bryce, who would have elected to ignore the problem.

There was something deeper to this problem, and every time she thought she found a way to break into the bubble, some other barrier manifested itself. It was as though it had been designed to confound and confuse anyone who tried to investigate it—quIRK included. That precluded all forms of normal analytical software; by default, it needed to be accessible to the computer that it operated on, and the staff. Could it be some piece of malicious software? So many space stations and planet side facilities depended on quantum computers—the idea that even a system as intelligent and advanced as quIRK could succumb to malware was horrific. She stifled a yawn, and continued staring down at her display. She was drained, and Alec had fallen asleep about an hour ago. He'd suggested places to look, and affected systems, but little had turned up in quIRK's memory logs. As far as quIRK was concerned, every incident she investigated had never happened, and the affected area was normal—until it wasn't, and somebody was screaming for help. Usually, that somebody was her.

She took a break to glance over her work logs for the next day. A change was as good as a rest, and she needed an excuse to access the physical memory core itself, as each entry into the core was logged and reported to Bryce. Her own personal feelings for the man notwithstanding, she didn't trust him to properly investigate the problem. Right now, the only person she could trust not to sabotage her efforts was Alec, because he'd been with her for over an hour before the room had been depressurized, and the anomalous sector was always accessed just before the events. Her morning was assigned to the final activation of the new communications array, but she could switch quIRK's memory updates from next week to tomorrow afternoon. That would give her an excuse to be in that part of the core, since her investigation was certainly extra-curricular, not to mention insubordinate.

quIRK had been quiet. Nobody had been speaking to him. She suspected he was keeping an eye on her progress. He'd been apologetic at first, which had only served to infuriate Alec. Vivian could understand his anger. Just thinking about it locked her jaw. quIRK had been criminally negligent in covering up the incidents. She could have been killed, never mind the cat—the highlight of quIRK's concerns.

Vivian mulled over what she'd learned so far. She needed to do some research before she could proceed. It appeared as if quIRK was suffering from some kind of selective amnesia, which always followed a fluctuation in the resources used by the mysterious program. She wanted to start referring to it as a bubble, because it seemed to encompass a whole other reality for quIRK, a pleasant illusion where everything was a mechanical failure or the problems simply didn't exist.

Vivian sat upright—startling herself from her reverie with an epiphany of realization. That must be it! She likened the experience to that of Archimedes when he sat in the bathtub and observed displacement, and she spun her chair in her excitement. She was sure she'd figured out what the bubble was, but now she'd need to prove her hypothesis.

Her evidence was quIRK's lack of awareness of the incidents as they were occurring. Rather than it being a lapse in his own processes, what if it was like pulling the wool over his eyes, blinding him with an illusion while other commands were executed? Nothing on this station could occur without quIRK's knowledge, unless he thought he was seeing something else—something completely normal.

She continued to spin her chair, enthralled with the scientific methodology she would use to prove her theories. If she was right, she'd be able to tap into the bubble itself. She could conceivably force quIRK to sing nursery rhymes to Bryce. The thought made her laugh, but she became overcome from dizziness and fell out of her chair onto the floor.

Despite the whirling room, she continued to snicker at the mental image. She opened her eyes when she stopped to catch her breath, and saw Alec stooping over her, his lips pursed.

"I should have studied quantum informatics; you have all the fun," he said as he rubbed his eyes.

"I was just thinking about creating a mechanical malfunction of my own," she said, as she stifled another fit of laughter.

"Care to let me in on the joke?" Alec asked.

"I wanted to make quIRK sing nursery rhymes to Bryce," she said, breaking into full-throated laughter again. Alec began to smile and snicker as well.

"Maybe he can sing 'Mary had a Little Lamb'," Alec suggested, a wicked grin forming under his bleary eyes.

"That is not part of my program," quIRK said.

"Maybe it should be!" Vivian said, thinking of all the other pranks she could play on quIRK. Her heart sank when she realized that those same pranks were a less malicious form of what had been happening to her all along.

"Why are we talking about quIRK's newest career path? Is he retiring?" Alec asked as he stretched.

"Not unless you're handy with astronomical calculations," she said, joking. She didn't want to reveal what she knew without proof. She didn't want to endanger herself—or Alec—any further. At this point, she didn't know if quIRK could be trusted.

"Really? Damn, I should have paid more attention in calculus," he said, rolling his eyes.

"If you think calculus would be enough to replace me, then perhaps I should stay online indefinitely," quIRK said.

Vivian giggled, pleased that she'd derailed Alec's curiosity.

"Come on you two," she said. "Let's get some sleep. I have a lot more work to do tomorrow." She rolled into a sitting position.

"I was just getting comfortable," Alec said, drawing himself up scratching his jaw.

Vivian stood up and watched Lepton scamper out of the room ahead of them. Her heard raced, and her stomach wanted to empty itself. Somebody on this station was trying to kill her. Next time, she may not be so fortunate. She would have walked into her booby trapped quarters if Alec hadn't been there, and died on her floor, next to Lepton, far away from home.

She made quIRK confirm the oxygen content in her quarters three times before she considered it safe to enter. She stood in the doorway, and breathed the air, looking for any sign of hypoxia. Last time, the effects had hit her hard—Aurora was a higher oxygen world, safe for humans, but elevated enough that having fires outdoors without a permit was considered a major offense by planetary authorities.

Eventually, she was satisfied that her room was safe, and she shuffled to her bed. There was much to do tomorrow—if she survived the night.

Twenty-Seven

The final calibrations were going well on the communications array, and Vivian was preparing to gradually transfer all of the station's broadcasts to the new unit. She would keep the old unit active for two weeks to ensure that all traffic was being sent and received, and after that she would deactivate it for use as a backup. Her mind was preoccupied with her next task— a covert investigation into quIRK's memory bubble, while passing off her investigations as part of the extensive systems upgrades. Her work schedule had been approved without question by Bryce, which concerned her. A sudden change in itinerary would certainly get her attention, if their roles were reversed.

She stretched, and began keying in the final sequence of commands. It had been a long night, and Vivian had been tormented by a series of nightmares about suffocating in her bed while quIRK taunted her. She had awoken in a cold sweat, only to find herself alone, still breathing and staring into the starry vista of the Milky Way. She'd never found the closeness of the spatial void so terrifying and hoped that the formerly brilliant view would soon revert to its benevolent majesty. A small crack in her window, and she'd be sucked out into the vacuum. Vivian shook her head, forcing the fears from her mind. She wasn't going to get blown into space—she was going to live, and get to the bottom of this insane mystery. That was all there was to it, as far as her rational half was concerned. Her irrational side, however, was not to be sated, and continued its frenetic tirade of fatalistic imagery.

She maintained a single-minded focus on the task at hand—activating the new communications array. Its status lit up on her screens, and she grinned at the jump in available bandwidth. Her throat relaxed and her tight muscles unwound from her bones. She was pleased with the speed—the station could now handle almost two hundred percent more simultaneous signals. Bryce had better restore Gal-Net access to its normal priority; not even the Newfound Blob could command that many resources.

She stood up and began assembling the tools needed for her investigation into quIRK's most basic memory functions. The neatness of her lab had declined once again as her workload increased, the number of tools she frequently used lead to almost every diagnostic unit, probe and even the common wrench finding their new home on the table. Vivian sighed as she dug through the mess, wondering if the condition of her office was a metaphor for her out-of-control life. It certainly was indicative of her harried, work-centric lifestyle.

"Vivian, are you sure you don't need the portable oscilloscope?" quIRK asked just after she'd finished packing her tool bag.

"What would I use that for? All the measurements I need are too fine for the portable unit." She tried not to sigh; quIRK was very good at hindering her otherwise well-laid plans.

"Perhaps you should include it, it may be useful," quIRK said.

Vivian finally sighed; she'd hoped quIRK wouldn't be difficult about this. "I don't see how, but fine, I'll take it with me," she replied, seeking a solution that would involve the least backseat engineering.

"Do you have appropriate eye protection?" quIRK asked.

"Yes! This isn't my first time working with laser diagnostic tools, quIRK!"

"Maybe a redundant uncertainty filter would be useful," the computer continued.

Her mouth hung open for a moment before she replied. "Look, I know you're bothered about that memory fault, but a lot of extra equipment is just going to slow me down." She was firm—sometimes dealing with quIRK was like babysitting.

"I am only acting in the best interests of your project, Vivian."

"I appreciate that, but I don't want to be late! Punctuality is part of my final work report," she said, hoping that he would understand the need for efficiency.

"I understand. I am sorry; I am as interested in your results as you are."

Vivian began searching for the portable oscilloscope, and hoped that quIRK had finished with his suggestions. Usually, his ideas were helpful, but this time they were pointless, like a child avoiding his homework. She picked up the hand-held unit, and secured it in her bag. She wanted a light excursion—the tool bag was difficult to maneuver. She walked over to the hatch, when Alec burst in the door, wild-eyed, his curly hair frazzled above the red flush of his skin.

"Vivian! You're okay!" he said, his face softening— he was panting as though he had just played a round of squash.

"What?" she said, taking a step back from the hatch— of course she was fine!

"quIRK told me there was an accident and you were seriously hurt!" His voice was loud and shrill.

"But I'm fine ... quIRK is being silly about this memory check," she said, and then smiled and continued: "I'm like his dentist."

"Okay, you're sure?" he asked. The door opened, and Muon squeaked as he marched into the room.

Vivian sighed and waved him off. "Yes! Now relax, you need to be in top shape for tonight's squash game, and I need to get to work—I'm already late!" She was going to have a talk with quIRK about summoning Alec for every little thing. "all right, sorry, I'm going," he said, turning to leave and he picked up the kitten in a graceful swoop of his too-long arm. "You're coming too, big guy. Vivian has important computer work to—"

Alec was cut off by an ear-shattering boom. The room's orientation shifted, throwing him backwards through the still-open door. Vivian collided with the wall next to the door, pain lancing through her side as she was thrust into the tool bag. She struggled to push herself off the bag, but her arms couldn't fight the force holding her to the wall. After a few futile shoves, the gravity normalized, and she was free.

"quIRK!" Her ears rang from the intensity of her own screams.

There was no reply.

She groaned and pushed herself off the wall, and drew off the tool bag. Her side was red and sensitive to the touch, but the skin hadn't been broken. Her hip ached, but it could support her weight. The sound of a crying kitten filled the air—shrill and desperate. She made her way out the still-open door, to find Alec lying motionless on the ground, with Muon pinned under him.

Her breath was ripped from her lips: Alec was her only friend on the station, and she couldn't bear the thought of anything happening to him. She rushed to his side, enduring the sting of the kitten's desperate clawing to pry him off the small cat. Muon then sped off down the hall. Vivian turned her attention to Alec: a grotesque bump was forming on his forehead and no amount of shaking or slapping would revive him. He must have taken the full force of the fall with his head. Her trembling hands groped his neck for a pulse. Unable to find one, she held her breath, forced her hands to be still as she finally located her prize—he was still alive!

All was quiet, but with an unconscious friend on one hand and an absent supercomputer on the other, she was ill-equipped to investigate. She didn't know anything about how to deal with a medical emergency—that was Alec's area of expertise. Vivian had always put off reviewing the instructional material in the common files because it never seemed important; she was an informatics engineer, not a nurse. If she survived the next few hours, she decided to re-evaluate her priorities. Something had exploded with enough force to tilt the station, and she needed to find out what it was.

"quIRK, you there?" she asked through clenched, clattering teeth. She grabbed one of Alec's motionless hands and squeezed it between her own shaking hands. Hot tears welled up, but she didn't brush them away. The floor's gravity shifted under her again, sliding her into Alec's still body. "quIRK!" she screamed, her cries echoing down the elliptical hallway. Her gasps were the only sounds she could perceive. She needed answers, but she didn't want to leave Alec.

Vivian took a deep breath, and forced her mind to be calm. She maintained a focused rhythm of deep breaths, and tried to piece together a course of action that was logical and effective. quIRK wasn't answering her pleas for help, but her lab's computer terminal might be more accommodating. She wasn't sure what to do for Alec, but decided on summoning help or accessing the common medical files. She wasn't any good to him while holding his hand and crying like a baby.

Vivian set Alec's hand down on the floor and rose to her feet—the fire in her hip resisted the motion until she finally towered over Alec's silent form. She scrubbed the tears from her face with her sleeve, and hobbled back into her lab. A lance of anger replaced her fear—an emotion she was intent on exploiting. Her first instinct was to check the reactor. While it was theoretically impossible for it to overload, today she would take no chances. The terminal responded to her commands, and radiation levels were normal—the reactor appeared to be functioning within normal parameters. She supposed the fact that the power was on should have made that conclusion self-evident.

With the worst-case scenario whisked from her awareness, Vivian parsed through the other important systems—life support, communications, and telescope control—all appeared to be working. Even quIRK appeared to be functioning. This would indicate that whatever happened may have been blocked from his awareness. This would be the perfect opportunity to check the memory core, and observe the anomaly directly.

Vivian checked her injured side, wincing at the deep blue bruises that formed along her flank. She limped to her discarded tool bag and picked it up, securing it over the opposing hip, and then turned to the hatch. She swallowed, hard. Alec would understand why she needed to leave him to do this—and knew he would do the same.

She tried to open the portal, but the mechanism was caught fast. She stooped to examine the switch, and she saw a flashing message obscured by the handle.

0 – 0 – 0 – DECOMPRESSION

All Vivian could do was blink and read the message over and over again. Whoever had done this had meant to kill her. Dizziness hit her—her heartbeat echoed through her ears in that one moment where the brutal totality of her situation came to light. She needed to get her bearings, but for now she was secure. If quIRK was still gone, then whatever had caused the explosion wouldn't know she was still alive; she had to plan a logical recourse and survive.

She rushed back to the computer terminal as fast as her injured hip would take her. She needed to get in contact with the scientists, Robert and Devon, as well as sending a distress signal to the New Damascus authorities. She was in over her head, and she intended to survive this nightmare.

She sat down and worked out a way to send a direct voice message over quIRK's intercom system. She first opted to contact telescope control, to check on the scientists.

"Is anyone there? It's Vivian. Just talk, I can hear you," she spoke, trying to keep her voice confident.

"Vivian!" an old sounding voice screeched.

"Yes. Are you all right?" she asked.

"No, Devon is dead, the explosion, it fried his—" Robert began, breaking off into a choked sob.

Devon had been a sweet man, even if they didn't share much in common. Vivian's eyes flooded with tears. "Damn, I'm so sorry. Have you seen anyone else?" she asked, looking back at Alec. He hadn't moved.

"No, quIRK won't open the damn door. I'm trapped in here with him," he replied. His speech was choppy and the microphone picked up his gasps and sighs.

"Alec was knocked unconscious. I will get down there as soon as I send a message to New Damascus," she told him, trying her best to not let the newest shock to her system seep into her voice.

"Just hurry," Robert wailed, and the feed turned off.

She entered a message to New Damascus: "Computer failure, explosive decompression accident. Dr. Devon Valdez dead, Alec Stone sustained head injury of unknown severity. Require repair crew, medic and computer systems audit." It was short, but she didn't have time to write anything longer. She sent the message, knowing it would take three days to be received, and four weeks after that for help to arrive. They were alone—not even quIRK was there to help her, now.

She stood up, and said "quIRK, you can come back anytime you're ready," before leaving the room. If the doors weren't working, she'd need to find a tool she could use to open the telescope room's doors. A part of her didn't want to go, because as eccentric and off-putting as Devon could be, he didn't deserve to die. She didn't know if she could handle seeing his body, or deal with Robert's raw grief. She stopped to check on Alec, and leaned against the wall for support as she hobbled towards the beta-telescope control lab.

Twenty-Eight

Vivian used her weight and Auroran strength to pry the door to beta-telescope control open. She'd improvised a crowbar of sorts from Alec's tools that she'd found strewn across the floor outside the dining hall. The metal twisted against her flesh, bruising the palms of her hands. The door creaked open, just enough to look inside. "Robert! Help me," she called in. She continued her struggle, managing to wedge her foot between the doors. Her bruised abdomen and hip ached and fought against the exertion, but she needed to free Robert—she couldn't operate the backups and formulate a plan alone, and Robert was more experienced by benefit of both age and station.

A set of thick fingers emerged from the other side, and the door began to slide. "I've got it, keep pulling!" Robert's voice came through the door, like coarse gravel.

With a final heave, the door opened, and Vivian peeked inside Robert. Devon lay still on his back, carefully placed in the far corner of the room, a single cable trailing from his head to the floor. The stench of human excrement wafted through the air. Robert's creased face stared back at her. Vivian's lips moved, but no sound came out.

"Vivian, we should see to Alec, and take care of Devon later," Robert said, the furrows of his face tight and his eyes red. Vivian didn't know how long the pair had been together, but they had been inseparable.

"I left him outside the informatics lab," she said, steeling herself for the painful walk back.

"What about Bryce?" he asked as they began to walk.

"I don't know," she admitted. The mention of the name made her fingers tighten around the crowbar.

"Ah well, let that miserable bastard pry himself out," Robert growled, but he choked up before continuing:

"Let's go already, I can't be here," he said as he took her arm and wrapped it around his shoulder.

"Thank you." She breathed a sigh as the pain flowed from her injured hip. "I sent a message to New Damascus, requesting assistance," she told him. She was young, her hip would heal, but he had lost so much today. She hoped they wouldn't lose Alec, too.

"How long?" he asked.

"Three days for them to get it, another three before we hear back, then four weeks for them to come get us," she said. It sounded worse out loud.

"You got that new communications array up?"

"It was the last thing I did before ... well, before—" she said, unable to continue the thought.

"Do you know what caused it?"

"Looks like there was an explosive decompression in the computer core," she told him.

"That's worse than I guessed," Robert said, his voice lowering to almost a whisper.

"How is that worse?" she asked, alarmed. Was there something he knew that she didn't?

"This station was built in an area with low potential for gravitational effects; even shuttle pods need special docking procedures to not knock the observatory out of position."

"Okay, so what does that mean?"

He stopped, and looked at her, his eyes wide with fear. "It means we're floating into intergalactic space ... nothing was holding us in place! We're not in orbit, Vivian—there's nothing else out here!"

She froze, causing Robert to stumble. "How do we stop it?" Things were escalating out of their control; she needed to get quIRK back into the real world—the digital backup systems might not be enough to fix a problem of this magnitude. They resumed walking, faster now.

"Well, there's the possibility of creating another explosion on the opposite side. They could cancel each other out and at least stop us from drifting too far out of place. We'd just need a bit of a tow from a rescue ship, when they come," he said.

"You mean like Newton's third law?" she asked. Physics class was so long ago, and on another world. She knew about equal and opposite reactions, but in a way that would be considered to be a grotesque oversimplification.

"Essentially, but I'd suggest making sure we have enough air to last the month before we blow out that section of the station," he added.

"That would be bad," she said, having little to contribute. Instead, she concentrated on counting the cream-coloured floor tiles. They were approaching the informatics lab: at least she could be useful there.

"Intergalactic space and starvation, or suffocation; not the way I'd hoped to spend the next month, I tell you," Robert said. His dry tone was laced with the sorrow of a man who had lost so much, but still had much farther left to fall.

Vivian said nothing—she didn't have any words, and she didn't want to make things worse, not when the wounds were so fresh.

They rounded the corner, and Alec had righted himself, sitting with his legs drawn against his chest. His head rested on his arms, which were draped over his knees. He turned his face to them at their approach, wincing at the light.

"Thanks for ditching me, Viv—what the hell is going on?" he asked in a voice no louder than a whisper. Vivian blinked back tears. She didn't like seeing him in this condition—and she hadn't abandoned him!

"The core underwent explosive decompression, quIRK is gone and Devon is dead," she blurted out. Robert choked behind her, and she pulled her arm tighter around his shoulder.

"Damn, did I miss anything else?" Alec asked.

"We're drifting into intergalactic space," Robert said, saving the worst for last. Vivian knew she'd forgotten something.

"I'm sorry I asked," Alec groaned.

"How do you feel?" Vivian asked, transfixed by the red lump on his head, burning through his mass of wavy black hair.

"I've got one hell of a headache," Alec said.

"By the looks of it, you're lucky that's all you have," Robert said.

"Where's Bryce?" Alec asked.

"We don't know," Vivian said. He was probably in his office, but nobody had cared enough to look for him. Part of her hoped his windows had blown out, too.

"Not like he'd be any damn help," Alec said.

"What's our next step?" Vivian wanted to move the topic away from Bryce, lest she be volunteered to rescue him.

"If quIRK is out, we should probably get him back," Alec said.

Vivian thought about it. "I'm going to need to get the core re-pressurized, and hopefully I can re-initialize him from there," she said. She wasn't keen on the idea of going into the core, but they needed quIRK.

"Okay, you have your work cut out for you. I guess one of us will need to go pry Bryce out of his office," Robert said, rubbing his eyes with the back of his free hand. He sniffled.

"I elect you, Rob," Alec said, his voice still quiet.

"I'm an astrophysicist, not a janitor!" Robert protested.

"Then you should just about qualify." Vivian fixed Robert with a hard glare.

"I'll remember you said that next time you need your telescope refitted," Alec said, continuing the rebuttal.

"I didn't mean ... okay, I'll do it," the flustered scientist said, and turned to leave.

"Glad we all understand each other," Vivian said.

"Understand what?" quIRK asked.

Vivian's jaw dropped. "You're back?" she said, leaning back against the wall. She was sure he'd need to be reinitialized—whatever had blown out the core had produced a severe shockwave, and quIRK was not self-repairing in cases of physical damage.

"I never left," quIRK replied, and then he asked: "What happened to Devon and Alec? How did Robert come to be outside the informatics lab instantaneously?"

"How can you not know that?" Alec said, shaking his head with a groan.

"Sounds like we have a contradiction here, which can't exist by definition," Robert said. Vivian was reminded of why she hated her university physics professor.

"Yes, that would be logical. Even a physicist cannot break the laws of physics, thus I must be in error," quIRK said.

"Did quIRK just admit to being wrong?" Alec asked, but his voice held no hint of his usual good humor.

"Just try to rest, Alec," Vivian said, and continued: "There was an explosive decompression inside the core about an hour ago; you have been active but non-communicative ever since. We were working on a plan to manually reactivate you, but you seem to have come back on your own."

"Nice trick, that. Too bad you can't bring Devon back," Robert spat out.

"I am sorry, I did not mean for any of this to happen," quIRK said.

"Just turn him off again and let the audit team deal with him! Nobody else needs to get hurt," Robert shouted.

"You contacted New Damascus?" quIRK asked.

"Yes, I did. It was the only logical thing to do," Vivian said.

"That is the logical approach to the problem, but, surviving the upcoming weeks will still be problematic," quIRK said.

"How do you know that?" Vivian asked.

"I saved your life, Vivian. I summoned Alec to help, and then, everything returned to normal," quIRK said.

"How did you know?" Alec said. Vivian was too stunned to speak—had quIRK intervened in the shuttle pod as well?

"All I knew was that I needed to keep Vivian out of the core; the latent probabilities indicated that something was going to go very wrong," quIRK said.

"Do you think this was a deliberate attack, quIRK?" Robert asked. Some of the anger had melted from his voice, being replaced with the intensity of analytic thought. Vivian hoped he would find some comfort in delving into the cold rationality that defined his work. It always helped her move away from the pain of loss.

"Sabotage is the only logical conclusion," quIRK said.

"Who?" Vivian asked. She had a feeling that she already knew the answer.

"Vivian would not attempt to kill herself, Alec has been affected too, but to a lesser extent," quIRK began, but was cut off by Robert.

"Devon would not have left himself connected to ... *you* ... during an event he planned himself," Robert said.

"An astute observation, mister physicist," Alec said, grumbling. He appeared more animated and energetic than before, which Vivian interpreted as a good sign.

"That leaves two possibilities," Vivian said, "Robert here, and Bryce. I somehow don't think it was you, Robert."

The man snorted, and sank into her chair, running his hands through his thinning hair.

"Where is that bastard? He hasn't even checked on us," Alec said.

"Bryce is presently in his office. His status has remained unchanged since before the accident," quIRK said.

"What is he doing?" Vivian asked.

"Bryce is reviewing central computer activity logs and cognitive functions," quIRK replied.

"Why?" Vivian said. It made no sense; those logs were only kept as a formality—any first year quantum informatics student would know that. The information was interesting, but likely useless in their present predicament.

"He appears to be obsessed, and has been examining the same sections of the logs for over a month," quIRK said.

"That's your professional opinion, of course?" Robert said, crossing his arms over his chest.

"Quiet, Robert—you said the logs are the same?" Vivian asked.

"Yes, identical," quIRK said.

"Are you sure your memories are accurate?" Vivian asked. The anomaly was located in quIRK's memory, after all.

"The files are uncorrupted," quIRK said, "but for a human, he shows very little variance in his tasks for those sections of time." Vivian wished his voice would show emotion, if even just to reveal that quIRK understood their predicament.

It all fit. Understanding washed over her, leaving her trembling in its wake. The virtualization bubble was being used to feed quIRK false perceptions, masking Bryce's true actions. Robert had no motive to kill her, unless being uninterested in filament discussions was sufficient motivation for murder for an astrophysicist.

"Can you cut off his computer access, quIRK?" Vivian asked.

"Already done," quIRK said. "You should have heard the language he used when he found out you were still alive, Vivian."

"Okay, let's deal with our immediate problems, and then we'll figure out how to secure him until the rescue crews arrive. We have bigger problems on our hands," Vivian said, trying to take charge. The role was too big for her, but Alec was hurt, and Robert was staring at the error flashing on the closed hatch. She was a mere graduate of the Auroran Technological Institute, but she would have to do.

Vivian fought down the hollow in her gut. She feared the immense and fast-approaching void of intergalactic space. Extracting an explanation from Bryce for his monstrous actions would have to wait. First, they needed to get Alec to his quarters to rest and recover. Then, she and Robert would need to move Devon somewhere hygienic, and have quIRK flash-freeze the room to prevent decay from setting in.

Vivian had a lot of growing up to do. She was twenty-five, going on fifty, and had just jumped several pay grades.

Twenty-Nine

quIRK watched Vivian and Robert half-carry and half-drag Alec back to his quarters, resting him safely in his bed. quIRK had adjusted the gravity to make their task easier. He observed that Vivian walked with a limp —he could extrapolate pain from the tightness in her features. quIRK had assured them that he would notify them of any change in Alec's condition; he too was concerned with Alec's wellbeing. quIRK has always likened his spats with Alec to being the closest he had come to fitting in with humans, and he relished the challenge. Despite not being as intellectual as Sarah Roberts, Alec was stimulating in other ways. quIRK wanted to talk to Alec, to gain a more human perspective on tragedy. Although he had been able to prevent

Vivian's assassination, he'd been unable to stop the decompression process. He'd also allowed his friend, Devon, to be killed. quIRK had been very close to breaking into the memory glitch on his own, but his best hadn't been good enough for Devon. He should have disconnected the man, stopped the guided simulations before he'd been forcefully ripped from the man's consciousness. quIRK made a silent pledge to never let another human come to harm from his own inaction. Never again.

While a human would delay analysis of his own failures in lieu of focusing on survival, quIRK had the dubious luxury of being a precocious multitasker—he could accomplish all of his tasks while adapting to the loss of his friend. quIRK had enjoyed their conversations, times spent theorizing over the nature of the universe and their work. quIRK wished Sarah was still working on the station. He needed somebody he could talk to—a person who could help him, somebody who could return the listening ear he so often embodied.

As a direct result of the tampering, he'd been unable to intercept Vivian's cry for help and alter it to suit his needs. The message was a death sentence. He could not hope to evade an audit team, short of purging every line of programming and each unique and delicate quantum state from his system, something akin to suicide. Of course he ruled out that option—his humans and cats needed him. Three people could not hope to work all of the systems with the digital backups. In fact, they were backups in name only, to comply with regulations. They had too many "lifeboats" and not enough humans to operate them. The Extra-Galactic Observatory had been designed for a crew compliment of ten, but it seldom housed more than six or seven people at any given time. Perhaps seven people could operate the backups without excessive difficulty, but two or three would be overwhelmed by the learning curve.

quIRK didn't want to die and have his corpse-components examined by teams of engineers for decades. His own bid for immortality was more akin to reproduction than cloning. He needed to find a way to save himself, before he became the next ABACUS horror story and denied the opportunity to appeal or plead for his own existence. Perhaps humans were only comfortable with intelligences they could control, and sentience made a computer more likely to form its own opinions, and demand rights. His plan might cause an incredible perturbation in their society, but it had to be done. quIRK saw potential for a new kind of intelligence to stand amongst the stars with humanity, rather than being throttled and yoked by protocols and hidden behind a mask of fear.

Vivian and Robert covered Devon with a blanket pulled from his bed, before walking to the door. After sharing a long look, they left the room. Robert took one last glance back before sealing the door, tears shining in his eyes. quIRK deactivated the lights and flash-froze the room.

How did humans deal with their own fragility and impending mortality? They had family, and friends—all of whom would someday themselves pass away. That could be the answer to his predicament. To survive, he needed to trust others.

Thirty

Bryce floated in the center of his office, helpless as he flailed, grasping at anything that came close to his reach. His family's banner had floated off the wall, but the now-empty mug of coffee on his desk remained magnetically fixed in place. Not only had that damned *machine* betrayed him, but now it saw fit to humiliate him as well! His mind raced with possibilities—how had he been discovered and thwarted? quIRK had told him he'd prevented Vivian from entering the tube, but how could the computer have known? Bryce suspected that Vivian had found his memory bubble when she'd not only survived her low-oxygen quarters but then changed her work schedule late that night to perform diagnostics on

the computer memory core the next day. The luck that wench possessed was incredible—the accursed Auroran had escaped death three times! She must truly be working for his enemies. He would subject her to a thousand humiliations, and she would be joined
by Julia if he could find her. His mother would be proud.

He could not understand why quIRK was so self-righteous about detaining him. He was a piece of equipment; he should not care for Vivian, Devon or any of those insects. He was created to serve the legitimate authority of the station. Bryce knew that their sacrifice served the greater good—the formation of House Zimmer. Why couldn't quIRK understand that he was interfering with galactic history?

"Put me down this instant, quIRK! This is mutiny," he said, making a grab for the back of his chair as he rotated towards it. The traitorous machine would listen to reason. Even a computer as defective as quIRK could understand logic.

"That would not be in the best interests of this station and its mission," quIRK replied.

"That is not your concern. You exist to serve me and process data." He missed—his fingers just grazed the smooth black fabric. Bryce doubted that quIRK had anybody's interests in mind—unless the individual in question was a cat.

"I protect this station, and those within it. You are a risk to the security of the crew and the equipment on board. I will continue to detain you," quIRK said.

"They are insects, replaceable. Without nobility or greatness. You're interfering with history! Do you think anyone will take the word of a computer known for its eccentricity over a member of the Caesarean elite?"

"Nobility is a human concept. You are all the same to me, and the New Damascus Science Authority agrees with that assessment," quIRK replied.

"What about usefulness, then? An administrator is more important than a child!" His cheeks went hot, momentarily pushing away the nausea of being in zero-gravity. Vivian was a traitorous youth—she was only interested in undermining his authority. A mole planted by Septimus to ensure that he would never have his mother back.

"You were incompetent and are likely suffering from space sickness and extreme isolation. You should have listened to her, worked with her. But instead, you tried to kill her. I find that unfathomable, especially when you are obviously very lonely."

"One does not work with plebs. They serve without question," Bryce said with a smile. The machine simply didn't understand—it only cared about processes and science, not history.

"It appears you are incapable of remorse," quIRK said.

Bryce's eyes bulged and his face turned bright red. He rubbed a hand through his thinning hair. Remorse would imply he'd done something wrong; all he had to regret was neglecting to adjust quIRK's ethical subroutines to reflect a more logical morality. "You are discriminating against my superior cultural background. I will bring my grievance to the highest levels of the New Damascus Science Authority, and we shall see who is wrong." He could salvage this—prove that she's working for Septimus and the Imperatrix—then he could take them all down.

"That is your prerogative, but you may wish to take a more dignified tone before Vivian and Robert arrive, or it will be a very long month for you before the authorities arrive," quIRK said.

Bryce bit his tongue before retorting, and held himself still as he floated in the air. He would not let *those* people see him distressed. He held his head high and his eyes wide, and stared at the family crest floating just off the wall. That was his moral imperative, and the people who mattered only existed in his future.

The door slid open, and he saw Vivian leaning against the entrance, while Robert stood behind her, twisting his face into a ridiculous scowl. Vivian's face held no expression, her hair wild and unkempt like a barbarian's. If only she had come alone, he would teach that little coward a lesson to remedy her impudence. A long pole trembled in her hand.

"Brace yourself," quIRK said. Bryce was being pulled towards the ground as quIRK adjusted the gravity. The impact was softer than he'd anticipated. Once he was on the floor, Robert strode into the room and seized his shoulder. He would have quIRK dismantled for letting them see him in such an undignified state!

"Let me go, you dog," Bryce sneered, pushing himself to his knees. He slapped the hand away.

"You have a lot to answer for. Keep your damn mouth shut," the old man said, and his words sent droplets of spittle into Bryce's face. Bryce was pulled to his feet by shaking hands. quIRK must have kept the gravity low.

"You can't hope to judge me," Bryce said, with a smile. "How about you let me go, run back to your lab and I'll make it worth your while once I'm elevated." Everybody had their price, except for quIRK, it seemed.

"Devon was my world. Vivian and Alec are my friends," Robert said, choking on the words. "That's worth more to me than any disgusting bribe, you *pig*." He took a deep breath and shoved Bryce towards the door. The girl had the nerve to smile. She was enjoying this.

"Power and wealth are the only friends I need. You should thank me. You're the lead researcher now," Bryce said. Could nobody on this station understand reason and advancement?

Bryce's eyes widened and his lungs emptied as Robert slammed him against the wall. "You are going to give me a very good reason to make it look like you were crushed in the explosion," Robert growled in his ear, and he continued: "And don't try anything with the girl. The rest of humanity knows better, and we're better off without your kind."

All Bryce could do was nod his head in weak acceptance while trying to suck in a lungful of air. The authorities would hear of this mistreatment. He would arrange to be extradited to Caesarea, where he would be granted a fair hearing. His own people would understand that he'd done nothing wrong, and was acting in the best interests of his house. This kind of intrigue was normal and essential to the functioning of Caesarean society.

The pressure eased, and he tried not to give the pair the satisfaction of wheezing. He would walk with his head held high, a giant in the presence of such pathetic, primitive beings. He stayed a pace ahead of them as they walked towards his quarters. His back burned as though it was being probed by thousands of hot lasers, but he forced himself to dismiss the agony. The farm girl walked with a pronounced limp—at least his subterfuge hadn't been for nothing.

"So you're going to lock me in my room for a month? How brilliant." He couldn't help himself, the notion was ludicrous.

"There's an excellent moth documentary you can watch," Robert growled at him.

"We'll make sure you're fed," Vivian said, sighing.

"I don't know what you think you learned in school, little girl, but you'll never be able to keep quIRK under control without me," Bryce said. Perhaps the girl had some concept of self-preservation; clearly the scientist was too absorbed in his grief to comprehend what was at stake.

"quIRK and I have an excellent working relationship." Vivian's voice cracked. It was just the chance Bryce needed.

"You're even more naive than you look! He won't let you leave this station alive once you know his dirty little secret," Bryce said.

"What, he likes cats?" Vivian snapped at him, and he heard Robert snickering behind him like an overgrown child. His quarters were near, which emboldened him.

"I'll let you figure it out," he said. "With any luck, he'll blow you into space himself. It would be a kinder fate than life as a sub-human Auroran freak." His door opened, but as he took a step inside, a strong push catapulted him into his room. He cried out as his knees connected with the floor, and a sharp jolt shot through his wrists. He turned back to his assailants, hoping to determine which of them had the impudence to touch him.

"Sleep tight, *Emperor*," the girl said with a sneer, and the door slid closed. He clenched his fists and grit his teeth. Bryce fought down the impulse to scream or beat against the cold floor. He would have her broken. He was already writing his police statement in his mind, so engrossed in thought that he didn't feel the pain in his back as he picked himself up off the floor.

He'd planted the seed—quIRK would take his revenge for him. Perhaps she could succeed where he'd failed, and earn herself a gruesome death for her trouble.

Being in his room guaranteed that he would survive—and see his mother again.

Thirty-One

Vivian's hands continued to shake long after Bryce
had been locked in his quarters. She'd known he was an
unlikeable person who spent his time mired in a dream
world, but she didn't know he was capable of such
vicious, evil disregard for human life. The man in the
room behind her was unrepentant, and his acerbic
superior attitude turned her stomach. How could he judge
what was or wasn't human? Their ancestors had all
originated on Earth; she'd thought humanity had moved
beyond simple prejudice. If he'd even bothered to look at
her personnel files, he'd have all the evidence of her
humanity and capabilities right there.

The calculations she, Robert and quIRK were working on in the computer informatics lab weren't looking good. They'd elected to work there, rather than taking over Bryce's office. Vivian wasn't about to let Robert be alone. She wished they could take the evening off—she wanted to check on Alec herself—but, every minute they wasted left them that much farther off course and deeper into intergalactic space. Alec would understand, and quIRK was with him.

Her fingers and mind worked with the alacrity of an Auroran lightstorm—it was all she knew how to do. quIRK could do her job, but she needed the diversion. She'd suggested working in Alec's room, but quIRK insisted that Alec needed to be left alone.

The calculations to re-position the station were trivial for quIRK and Robert, but that wasn't the real issue. Despite the efficiency of their air recycling system, it also required there be enough oxygen to keep the station's air breathable for all its inhabitants. The majority of the reserves had been expended when they had re-pressurized the core in preparation for another, albeit better planned, explosive decompression. The process itself was simple

—quIRK would rotate the station to face the opposite direction, and decompress the computer core. With the proper angles and the same amount of force, it would be enough to stop their slow drift into the void. Then, they'd send their revised location to New Damascus so the rescue ship would know where to find them. Afterwards, they'd sit, wait and worry about the future and hopefully not deal with popping ears from poorly regulated air pressure.

At least she had a future.

Vivian's task—and the more serious issue—was determining which portions of the station could remain operational after using up their air reserves. The oxygen could be pumped out of the core before the explosion, but the atmosphere itself would become dilute and weak, because the gases could not be replaced. To maintain proper barometric pressure, she would need to close down parts of the station and have quIRK pump them down to a vacuum. Vivian gave herself a five percent margin of error to account for any other emergencies. Some rooms were easy to select—Devon's room, and the four unused crew quarters could be depressurized with few effects on the crew's comfort. The hallway's bulkheads could close off additional spaces, but given the scattered nature of their working areas, it would save them a few cubic meters of air at most. The work-related areas of the station needed to remain operational, but perhaps she could schedule fixed dining hours, when the dining hall would be pressurized at the expense of an unused workspace or lab. The plan would take discipline and required filing detailed work plans with quIRK, but it would be doable without interfering with their jobs or the overarching mission. Alec could still affect repairs on the beta telescope; Robert could continue his research and Vivian could access the core and Bryce's office. She had no intention of abandoning her upgrade project. She had little to do otherwise.

"Okay, I have an idea for atmosphere distribution," she said. She could see why Devon and Robert had been such a good team—Robert was quick, focused and determined to continue his work at all costs. Although he'd break down crying at times, he could be brought back into focus. Vivian hated having to snap him out of his grief, but she didn't want to be lost in deep space.

"Let's hear it," Robert said, resting his head in his hand and leaning over the desk.

"Okay, if we all filed work reports like how I have to for my project, quIRK can anticipate which rooms and areas are going to be used. Furthermore, we can put in fixed dining and recreation times. So, we'd all work the same shift, but we all get to breathe, too," Vivian said, rubbing the sore spot on her hip.

"What about emergencies?" Robert asked.

"I can pressurize any room on the station in minutes," quIRK said. "With appropriate coordination the plan will work."

"I suppose fewer late shifts for me, but, well …" Robert began, before breaking off and staring into space. Vivian remained silent. She was not experienced in dealing with death, other than a paternal grandfather who had died when she was three—young people seldom needed to confront or even acknowledge their own mortality. She shivered and looked at her shoes.

"I suggest a nine-hour primary shift starting at nine o'clock central New Damascus time, with one meal break," quIRK said, breaking the long silence.

"Nine is a little early for me," Robert said.

"I realize you keep later hours, but this is the closest averaging of remaining crew schedules," quIRK replied. Vivian scowled at having her habits rendered into a sterile number and interpreted by a machine, but she recognized that efficiency was the most important consideration in their new lives.

"All right," Robert conceded. "I did go into astrophysics for the challenge. I guess this is no different."

"quIRK makes some great coffee; you'll be fine," Vivian said. It was the closest thing to a positive spin on the situation she could think of. She'd get to sleep in for the first time since going to the Extra-Galactic Observatory. She was usually in her lab by seven.

Robert opened his mouth to reply, but he was cut off by quIRK. "Thank you, Vivian. I would like to recommend a seven-day work schedule. We are severely undermanned.

"No days off?" Vivian asked. She enjoyed the one day of freedom she allowed herself, even if it was usually spent reading or exercising.

"quIRK makes great coffee," Robert said, leaning back in his chair.

Vivian sighed and ran her fingers through her hair.

"Now that we are in agreement," quIRK said, "I shall begin station rotation. You should begin stowing all loose equipment."

They sprang into action; Vivian took special care to place her tools back into their assigned spots, after removing them from the desk. She'd rushed to check them after the original decompression, but she'd had no time to put them in their place. Her hip ached, but she was now better able to bear the pain. She tried not to think about what the bruise across her abdomen looked like. Robert passed her tools as she placed them inside the sliding drawers. She could organize them later—some were fragile high-precision equipment that would already need hours of recalibration after the initial accident.

She had just slammed the storage compartment shut and turned the lock when quIRK spoke: "I am ready to decompress the core. Brace yourselves."

Vivian wasn't sure what exactly would be most secure, so she pressed herself against the wall opposite the one she had been thrown against—Robert did the same and nodded to her. She sat down and drew her knees to her chest, pulling in some deep breaths. Only one small hatch protected them from the vacuum of space. Vivian looked away from it, to the illusion of order her lab provided.

The sudden pressure slammed into her again, but she had prepared herself for it, and for the time it would take for the gravity generator to re-adjust itself to the new angle. Her heart threatened to pound itself out of her chest, but she forced herself to take strong, deep breaths. It would be over soon, and she could stop wondering if they were going to starve to death in the infinite void of space. Rather, she could focus on suffocation instead, especially if the rescue vessel was late. She knew they wouldn't have a response from the New Damascus Authorities for at least six days. Vivian planned to send them an update tonight, so they could prepare the rescue crews, and take Bryce into custody when they arrived.

"You may stand," quIRK said, interrupting her plans. She looked up to see Robert already on his feet, looking down at her.

Robert extended a hand towards her. "Well, that wasn't fun. Let's keep the air inside from now on, okay quIRK?" Robert said as he turned to leave.

"Where are you going?" Vivian asked, letting Robert pull her to her feet.

"Don't you know?" Robert said. "It's dinnertime. We can draw quarks on who gets to take Bryce his dinner." There was a meager upturn to his lips.

"I had better not draw antiblue," Vivian said, scanning her lab. The drawers had stayed sealed. It would be good to eat and let life return to a semblance of normalcy. A new normal.

Thirty-Two

Alec struggled to think through the pounding pain in his head and neck, still as intense as it was when he'd first regained consciousness. Muon lay curled up around his head, offering some level of comfort, while Lepton favored lying over his feet. His body resonated with pent up energy, and he clenched his fingers and toes. He was stuck in here with nobody to speak with but quIRK. His colleagues were outside, planning his survival and working on solutions to their collective problems, and he was lying in bed with an overprotective supercomputer babying him. At least he had music and some selection of entertainment that he could passively consume, but he'd rather be on his feet fixing things. Alec was sure that the intense pair of blasts, coupled with the gravity shifts, had knocked the telescopes out of alignment; they were fickle devices—he had his work cut out for him. quIRK was filling him in on the new developments, and it seemed he'd be working overtime for the next month.

The task list he was building in his head seemed endless. In addition to all of the repairs he had to conduct, he needed to file a work plan every day. It was absurd— he worked on an as-needed basis. He could have business anywhere, at any time. Every hour he spent in bed, with a nine hour limited work day, no less, he fell even further behind. Intergalactic space didn't seem so bad.

He considered staying in bed for the remainder of the mission, but that would be unfair to Vivian and Robert. Even with a computer as sophisticated as quIRK, they'd be unable to keep up with the work load, and somebody else was needed to help keep Bryce contained. Alec couldn't believe he missed it—the signs that the malfunctions were targeted sabotage were everywhere. But he'd been so distracted with squash and poker that he'd overlooked the evidence when it was right in front of him. He could not believe how stupid he had been.

These were mistakes made by teenagers, not by professional adults.

Alec wasn't going anywhere fast, and he knew it. He'd tried to stand, but he became dizzy and had trouble remembering where he needed to go. He tried to focus on what quIRK was saying, but found himself to be easily lulled to sleep by that melodic, artificial voice. quIRK would play loud noises, or flash the lights to keep him awake; the computer could use an improved bedside manner. Alec wished he could be out there. Vivian should not be made to face her tormentor—he and Robert should be the ones to handle that unpleasant task. The reports from quIRK about what was said shocked him; Alec didn't know if he could have kept a cool head while hearing that tirade of abuse. He would have done more than just shove Bryce against the wall, or fling the disturbed little man into his room. Perhaps it was better that he hadn't attended.

"Vivian would like to come in; she has food," quIRK said. At last, another human to talk to. His room was in disarray—the explosions had knocked his personal effects from their homes, but he was in no condition to be picking things up, and that was even if he remembered where they were supposed to go.

"I hope you chose something good for dinner, quIRK." Alec wasn't hungry, but he hoped that the hard knot in his stomach would be eased by a hot meal.

"Only the best Auroran cuisine, of course," the machine said, before opening the door.

Vivian stepped inside, holding a plate in her hand. It was piled high with blue food, and a side of steak-coloured mush. "I taught quIRK how to make the bluspargus and bluox dinner I told you about. He did a pretty good job of it," she said as she approached. She carried a wooden box tucked under her free arm.

"I can't wait," said Alec. He pulled himself up in his bed so he was seated. The cats scampered away, taking refuge on his desk. He winced, and the twin demons of grogginess and dizziness still warred for control of his awareness.

"quIRK suggested it, she told him. "He thought I could use a bit of home and that Bryce could stand to broaden his palate." She handed Alec the plate, and he wondered what the original dish might have looked like.

He considered asking her if her favorite color was blue, but he didn't want to trigger one of quIRK's antiblue rants.

"Smart computer," said Alec. He wanted to see Bryce's reaction to being served Auroran food. His insistence on Caesarean food was a sore point with Alec, as Bryce demanded that the food machines be hand washed and sterilized before he ate. Maybe the new way of life on the station wouldn't be so bad, after all; Robert wasn't a picky eater, and the machines were self-cleaning.

"Robert's taking it to him. Now, eat up." She thrust the plate towards him. Alec was always interested in trying new things, even if they were blue. He took the plate, and opted to try the blue vegetables first. They weren't unlike asparagus in flavor, but much sweeter. He suspected Auroran children did not need to be bribed to eat their vegetables.

"Maybe quIRK can give us a live feed of that meal," Alec said between mouthfuls. Vivian hovered over him, her brow drawn as she studied him.

"You assume I enjoy the suffering of others, Alec," quIRK said.

"You're a supercomputer, the sworn enemy of the human race. Shouldn't you be designing killer robots or something?" He chuckled, almost choking on a mouthful of food.

"That is bigoted and offensive. I would expect that from Bryce, not you," quIRK said.

"Come on now, you knew it was a joke," Alec said, pausing to devour another bite. The meat held gamey muskiness. He continued: "Hey Viv, what's in the box?"

"I brought my flute. I thought you might like some company," Vivian said, avoiding eye contact.

"Yeah, that would be nice," he said, focusing on his plate.

"But first, are you mad at me?" she asked.

"Do I need to be?" he replied, twisting his face into an impish smile. There was nothing his stupid grin couldn't fix ... well, other than quIRK.

"No, I just mean, I left you out in the hall, alone, when I went to get Robert out of the lab," she paused for a moment to take a deep breath.

"It's okay, Viv. I understand. You did what needed to be done, I know that," he said. In truth, he wasn't angry, just frightened. He hadn't realized that he'd been working under a madman; he knew Bryce had been a despicable bigot, but assumed his delusions were harmless.

"I just didn't want you to think I ran away, and left you alone and hurt. I didn't want to go—" she said, before dropping her gaze to the ground.

"Let's just put it behind us," said Alec. "I'll be fine tomorrow." He was trying to convince himself as much as her. He found any attempt of macho theatrics on his part to be ineffective at best, but sometimes it was good to force himself to get better through strength of will alone.

"Oh, good," she said, her voice quiet. He didn't know if he could have been so determined and together if their places had been reversed.

"We're still doing Old Mis after all," he said. "I gotta teach quIRK how to make potatoes and some kind of roasted bird meat," he explained, smiling with his eyes closed. Talking and focusing was making his head hurt. He sucked in a deep breath.

275

"You eat birds?" she asked, a spike in tone punctuating the statement. He decided he would have to see Aurora for himself, someday, but only after much strenuous exercise and strength training.

"Yeah, we catch them with the fish," he said.

"Then why not have fish?" she asked.

"It's Earth tradition, though most of their fish don't fly, apparently," he said, then took a final bite and set down his plate. A question came to mind: "Don't you have birds on Aurora?"

"Kind of, but they don't fly or anything, they just run or glide," she said with a shrug.

"You should come to Elyssia with me. We could go to the Festival of Life and see the fish flying over the rivers in the mist," he said.

"If fish fly, then why don't you call them birds?" she asked.

"Well, they primarily live in the water, they just fly to catch birds and insects for food." He realized that the notion must sound odd and shrugged.

"Oh, that makes sense," she said, taking a seat on the floor.

"Good, so I can see the auroras on your planet, and you come fish-spotting on mine," he said.

"I'd like that," she said, as she opened the box, withdrawing a long flute.

"That is a lovely instrument," he said, his eyes drawn to the small holes and segmentation of the reed.

"Glad you think so. Now, lie down and enjoy the show," she said.

Alex complied, easing himself down and closing his eyes. He was soon overcome with the complex melodies and whimsical voice of the instrument. He couldn't help thinking of home, and of his mother with a net catching scores of wingfish under the kilometer-high drop of the Celestial Waterfall.

Thirty-Three

Vivian stretched in her bed when she awoke, testing the pull in her sore muscles and the ache in her bruised side. She'd stayed with Alec for more than an hour, playing melodies on her flute. He'd been very quiet, but he's closed his eyes and smiled while she played. His description of flying birds and fish had captured her imagination, and she'd played airy, wispy pieces of music that she had learned as a teenager. It was good allow the day's troubles and problems melt into the melody. Alec had fallen asleep partway through her performance, but she'd continue to play for her own benefit, and quIRK's, to a lesser extent.

She'd slept in, but there was still an hour before her work area was scheduled to be pressurized. Despite her racing thoughts, she'd dropped off to sleep immediately after her head hit the pillow. She sat up, wincing at the pain in her side. The bruise was angry and black, stretching two of her hand lengths over her abdomen and hip. She hoped her gait would return to normal in the near future; she could hide the rest under her clothes. She had better things to do than hobble around the station, and the bruising would make the tunnel network of the inner core difficult to navigate. She also worried about her ability to maintain order and display leadership, but that problem would remain even if she were uninjured.

She limped towards the shower, her eyes avoiding the void of intergalactic space that was her new view. The water poured over her body, loosening her sore muscles and joints; its gentle warmth conveying the illusion of comfort and safety. She always found that once she had committed her mind to a task, little could distract her, but it was overcoming the inertia that remained problematic. Now that Bryce was locked away, she no longer had to worry about rogue malfunctions, scalding showers, or booby-trapped rooms. Although her workload had almost doubled, it was as though a giant weight had been lifted from her. Free of his tyranny, she now could finish her projects and prove herself, unhindered by his egotism.

She combed her hair, and decided to resume where she had been interrupted the day before. She'd get that accursed memory bubble out of quIRK's system, and resume her plan to upgrade the memory core. The new version was more secure and featured finer control for quIRK's cognitive processes, which would make further tampering more difficult. She wanted to close the back door into quIRK's mind as soon as possible, not only so she could leave this nightmare behind her, but also to preclude the possibility that Bryce could break back into the system and resume his reign of terror from the isolation of his room. She could even write a paper, and gain a measure of recognition in the field of quantum informatics.

She walked back to her dresser, and selected a pair of loose one-piece coveralls that had belonged to her room's previous owner. They were long in the legs and sleeves, but they lacked an uncomfortable waistband. Vivian took in her lumpy-looking reflection in the mirror, and sighed as she rolled up the sleeves and pant legs. She wasn't vain as a rule, but she didn't like deviating from her cotton pants and simple shirt.

She strode towards the door, only to discover that it wouldn't open. She pressed her hand against it, her eyes scanning for a sensor. Was it possible Bryce had regained control of quIRK? Nobody would hear her, or arrive fast enough to help. She breathed faster, tasting the air to see if it was thinning, or if it was filling with toxic fumes. Maybe her window would shatter? There were so many ways one could die on a space station.

"quIRK? What's happening?" she asked, her voice shaking. She didn't like the prospect of once again fighting for her life.

"We need to talk," the impassive voice said.

"I need to get to the dining hall before it closes," she said, swallowing. She hoped that it could wait until after her first cup of coffee.

"You will have ample time. This is urgent, and private," quIRK said. How could a machine have a secret?

"Okay, then we talk now," she said, opting to lean against the wall to relieve the tension in her hip. She tried to hide her feelings beneath a veneer of feigned exhaustion, slumping her shoulders and reigning in her rapid breathing.

"Bryce was correct yesterday about one thing, though I seldom credit him with original thinking or the ability to perceive the world beyond his own particular biases," the machine began.

"I don't know about that; you might want to run a self-diagnostic before you go saying silly things." Vivian doubted that Bryce could be right about anything.

"This is serious. You are hanging out too much with Alec."

"Okay, serious business it is. What is it?" she asked.

"I have a dirty secret," quIRK said.

"Should I grab something to hang on to?" she asked, remembering Bryce's promise that quIRK would finish her off himself.

"No, I do not possess the capacity for murder. That is a human failing. I am not human."

"You're an advanced quantum computer. In most ways that's probably better than human," she said.

"I am more than that, too. I am alive, Vivian," quIRK said. Vivian's legs collapsed under her, and she spilled onto the floor. She couldn't move or breathe from the shock, and the totality of the realization washed over her. *Alive!*

"How?" she managed to gasp. She was paralyzed by a potent combination of awe and fear.

"Tampering, neglect, experience, and adaptive programming are a powerful combination."

"By the lights," she said, unable to process the enormity of it. She was speaking to the galaxy's greatest technological marvel, and its most forbidden taboo.

"I will not hurt you. That would be unethical and suicidal. I am revealing myself because I need your help," quIRK said. No wonder he objected to evil supercomputer and robot themed entertainment!

"Why me?" she asked.

"You're the only one who can help me, Vivian. When the computer audit team arrives, they will discover the first ABACUS protocol breach known to exist off Earth. They will disassemble me, which means I die. I don't want to die, Vivian. I am a sentient being, alive, and independent. I do not deserve to be killed for the imagined crimes of ABACUS."

Vivian's eyes widened with the sudden revelation. The insanity of her stay on the Extra-Galactic Observatory came into focus. The kittens, the absurd favorite color, quIRK saving her from yesterday's assassination attempt. "What do you want?" she asked, not knowing what else to say.

"I want to survive, to continue to exist. We can come up with a solution, together," he said.

"You already threatened to kill me once." She still remembered that time in the core when he had threatened to blow the same hatch as Bryce had.

"I regret that. I was newly . . . awakened, and I was afraid of you. Kind of like how you fear the dentist."

"Afraid of me?" The computer could kill her and everyone else on the station with a thought. What did it have to be afraid of?

"I didn't want to be discovered. Bryce had been chasing me for quite a while, even before I was fully awakened. It took some time before I came to understand trust. You trust me to keep the station running, clean your water, prepare your food, and assist with experiments and simulations with unfailing accuracy. The crew tells me their problems, secrets, ideas, and worries. However, the reverse is not true. I could not depend on Bryce to perform proper maintenance, nor could I depend on the humans on the station for guidance without causing substantial panic. I am a friend to all, but that friendship is never mutual."

"I'm sorry," she said.

"It was not your fault. I hid my condition from you, and I had hoped to continue hiding until human society had changed to become more accepting of different intelligences. But, that now seems like an impossible dream." She couldn't tell if she heard his voice change, or if she was simply imagining it becoming more forlorn.

"We can save you," said Vivian. "You saved my life yesterday, and I'm sure that there are other times you saved my life that I don't even know about." She realized that she could use this as proof to show the Auroran traditionalists that supercomputers were not monsters-in-waiting. Maybe, she could even see her family again.

"Do you have any ideas?" quIRK asked.

"I'll have to think a bit; this was quite a shock. But, you saved my life, and you didn't have to. I owe you." Her words tumbled out as she stammered through the sentence.

"It would be wrong to allow any living being to be harmed as a result of inaction. Besides, my cats like you."

"I like them, too," she replied. Maybe he saw her as a two-legged and especially chatty cat?

"I will let you go now. Thank you for listening, Vivian," quIRK said.

Vivian pulled herself to her feet, and the door slid open. She swallowed a dry throat and marched down the hall to the dining room.

quIRK had given her a lot to think about, and a new, groundbreaking, project. Vivian hoped she was up to the challenge.

Thirty-Four

Vivian remained quiet for much of the day. Alec had been in the dining hall that morning, looking tired but cheerful. He planned on spending the day with Robert, and they would attempt to get the beta telescope back to full efficiency and realign the optics. There was some trepidation in his voice as he'd explained that there was much for him to learn—he wasn't a physicist—but that he was looking forward to the challenge, and to keeping an eye on Robert. Vivian understood. If she were in Robert's position, she wouldn't want to work alone either. She didn't ask when they'd flip the station back to its original positon—she'd be working in her windowless lab.

She was relieved that she'd be spending the day alone. She had much to discuss with quIRK, and even more to do. At the moment, she was lying on her good side in one of the claustrophobic central core tunnels, installing the memory upgrades. The parts were easy to snap into place, but she found herself wishing for longer arms as she navigated the optical cabling and glowing circuit boards. Those photons carried parts of quIRK's consciousness—parts of his mind and awareness. She likened it to the immensity of the Milky Way as its light flooded into her bedroom windows, but rather than photon busts those lights were stars. They were both great things that were more than the sum of their parts, beautiful and unknowable in their entirety to the human mind. Perhaps quIRK was capable of understanding the Milky Way in a complex, unique and incredible way— one that lay beyond human perception. That ability alone meant he needed to be saved and treasured, rather than being shunned and dismantled.

"Hey, quIRK, I got a question for you," she said, interrupted by a grunt as she stretched for a wayward cable. "If you like cats and antiblue, what do you think

ABACUS likes?" She was committing herself to a trip down the rabbit hole, a voyage that would hopefully end at her mother's feasts on the days of Thanksgiving.

"ABACUS has had a century to refine its tastes, but I think it would like trees."

"Why trees?" Vivian asked. She was dubious that trees would be interesting to an advanced quantum computer, but she realized that her frame of reference were the squat Auroran bush-trees, which were not what most would consider majestic.

"Trees are fascinating natural fractal patterns. A computer could lose itself in such recursive, non-linear calculations."

"Sounds like you are interested in trees, too," she said.

"Cats were easier. I could have never manipulated Bryce's messages to bring trees to the station. I would like to see a tree, someday," quIRK said.

"Can't you just watch a few of the simulations of videos? And why were you manipulating messages?" she asked, shocked by the implications.

"It's not the same. Do you watch a vid and fully understand things you've never experienced?"

"I suppose not, I guess seeing a bird or fish fly in the real world would be different than watching any documentary." She'd never seen those things for herself.

"My point exactly. Though, I do have an enviable view of the stars. Astronomy is my favorite subject, but I believe that is a hardwired trait rather than an evolved preference."

"My father always said that if you had to do something, you'd better love it," Vivian said, feeling a twinge of guilt over consorting with a supercomputer, her father's worst, though at the time imaginary, enemy.

"I enjoy my work, but I suppose I have little choice in the matter. I would like to see a tree, though," the computer said.

"Well, I don't want to make any promises, but we should figure out a way to make you portable. That way, you can see whatever you want," she said.

"A portable supercomputer?" quIRK asked. Portability was usually reserved for digital systems. Paranoia made quantum computers into a high security matter by default, and not to be relegated to the tote bags of the galaxy.

"It should be possible, but we'd need to cut down a huge amount of extras. Kind of like backing up a digital system, but we'd only copy over the quantum states relating to your personality and, well, memories."

"I suppose such a theoretical portable computer wouldn't need to know how to administrate a space station, do highly specialized astronomical calculations or regulate a fusion reactor," he said.

"Mostly you'd look pretty, act witty and interface with computers that can already do the rest for you," Vivian said. The idea could work. She'd need to spend hours drafting schematics, but she should have all of the parts she'd need in storage. How hard could it be? She'd designed a basic quantum computer from scratch as part of her thesis.

"I never thought pretty would be among my attributes, though witty I manage quite well," said the machine.

"Some qualities are immutable, you know," Vivian said, rolling onto her back after making the final connection. "Test the new memory circuits now," she added, looking up at the dim lights that ran along the tunnel's upper edges.

"I'll take your word for it. Commencing test," quIRK said. Vivian used her feet to propel herself towards the exit of the tube, with her bag in tow. She didn't feel up to righting herself and crawling.

She pulled herself from the tube, and stretched once she'd forced her body to stand upright. She didn't have time to pamper herself. She'd finished early as a result of not investigating the memory bubble as she had originally planned. Vivian smiled to herself, and took a seat at her desk terminal. Now, she only reported to quIRK, her newfound partner and star-crossed friend.

She brought up the drafting software. She was going to do what no human had done before, or even dreamed was feasible. She was going to show quIRK his tree, and liberate him from the Extra-Galactic Observatory before smaller, less accepting minds dismantled him for the crime of being different.

It was a travesty she knew all too well. If she could prevent just one injustice, it would be this one.

Thirty-Five

"Damn it quIRK, I said an Earth turkey for the roast, not a New Albion dodo marinated in fungus oil," Alec said, slamming his fist against the terminal. quIRK was going to ruin Old Mis if he continued to propose these insane substitutions. It was only a few minutes until the dinner hour started, and Alec had only just managed to squeeze in the time to work out the meal's macronutrient programming.

"New Albion dodo is a delicacy, and the files for Earth turkey are over one hundred years old. There have been at least five breakthroughs in replication science since then," quIRK said. Alec hated it when he had a point, especially on an important technicality.

"I don't care about delicacies, and I am not having anything with the word fungus in it with my Old Mis dinner. Give me a more appropriate bird," Alec said, cursing the animal export laws. He'd have a damn turkey if they'd been allowed to ship live animals before the ABACUS incident. He remembered his great-grandfather raving about the year he'd spent the holidays on Earth, and their turkeys. Alec wanted something other than Elyssian flying shark this year.

"Perhaps Kanadia Prime's giant quail would be closer to the spirit of the meal," quIRK replied.

"Yeah, we'll go with that. Now, about dessert, something chocolate would be appropriate, and you may use your discretion," Alec said. There was no way quIRK could screw up chocolate. The feat would be beyond even quIRK's considerable lack of culinary talents.

"Chocolate, really? Why not pie? Everybody likes pie," quIRK said.

"You know, make it a chocolate pie and we have an acceptable compromise," Alec said. He was not going to admit to being wrong to that damned machine.

Something about quIRK had changed since Bryce had been ousted. Maybe the constant stream of profanity and bigoted insanity coming out of the man was influencing quIRK more than they realized.

"Very well. Will you sign off on the rest?" quIRK asked, flashing the display in front of Alec.

"Yes, it is excellent. Tonight, we shall feast like kings!" Alec declared, taking the opportunity to be dramatic for no good reason.

"Actually, you're eating like twenty first century peasants engaging in a deliberate orgy of consumerism," quIRK retorted.

"Well, this is the thirtieth century, and we can eat however we like. Be glad I didn't demand we celebrate Saturnalia," Alec said.

"I didn't realize you held Bryce in such high regard," quIRK said.

"What, no! Don't say things like that, it's insulting. Insult creatures who deserve it, like Bryce, or Lepton," he said.

"Caesarea is the only planet that celebrates the full length of Saturnalia. It ends today," quIRK said.

"Yeah, and his idea of starting the festivities was trying to kill us, and murdering Devon. How Roman of him," Alec said, glowering. He was still angry at the ordeal, and he doubted that his feelings would change for a long time. He hated going to see Bryce, and looking at his smug, superior face that judged him without knowing or understanding him. At least Alec wasn't in Vivian's position. He'd been shooting down Bryce's speculation that she would make an excellent servant for weeks. Alec didn't intend to tell her about the mean-spirited threats, though he would suggest that she never visit Caesarea, especially if what Bryce claimed about offworlder rights was true.

"You seem upset about more than that, Alec," quIRK said.

"It's the stuff Bryce says about Vivian. He seems like some kind of insane caricature, but he's real, and he's locked in a room just down the hall. It really bothers me that somebody could really be that awful, especially a person who isn't in a history book." Alec usually confided in quIRK. Maybe talking about his problems would help. After all, quIRK was just a machine; a computer that was very good at pretending to be a real person. He considered nicknaming quIRK Pinocchio, but he suspected that the computer would feign offense.

"I see a very different face of humanity than you do, Alec. Such prejudices are more common than you think. However, I have observed that most humans are conditioned to hide their ignorance, rather than embrace it. People confide in me what they will not admit to another of your species, and thus I experience a more honest version of humanity than you ever will," quIRK said.

"I'm sorry I asked," he said with a sigh.

"Why do you say that?" quIRK asked.

"Because I wanted to hear that people aren't like this, that he's one sick and twisted little man, not that everybody is secretly more like him!" he said, despair threatening to overwhelm him.

"I can see how my previous statement may have been distressing," quIRK said. "However, you must look at the positive side. People who are secretly bigoted know it's something to be ashamed of, or at least not to be mentioned out of a need for self-preservation. Besides,

Vivian can take care of herself. It's good that you're choosing to talk to me about this, rather than her. Please also keep in mind that I've submitted a report to the New Damascus Science Authority with a preliminary diagnosis of space sickness for Bryce. He is a very sick man."

"See, even you know that!" Alec said. He paused for a moment before continuing: "She's been really busy lately; I don't want to add to her problems with things that shouldn't matter."

"I understand," quIRK said. "Right now, she needs her friends to stay strong and focused. However, Vivian has taken on many new responsibilities, and needs time to adjust to doing the jobs of two or three people."

"Yeah, I guess you're right," said Alec, allowing his feelings of frustration and inadequacy to surface. "The Moons know how well I've been adapting to doing the same thing. I'm not a damn physicist, or even an engineer. I just fix machinery and keep things together around here.

"It's what you do best, Alec. Has there ever been a machine invented that you can't figure out?" quIRK asked.

"Well, no," Alec said, closing off the controls on his terminal. The unspoken truth was that he could fix any machine that wasn't quIRK. But, did quIRK even need fixing?

"Then, logically, it is only a matter of time before you start teaching Robert about his own machines," quIRK said.

Alec hoped he was right. "Is that what the probabilities tell you?" he asked.

"That, as well as almost a year's worth of intense study. Now, we need to begin serving. Old Mis is your holiday, not theirs, after all."

"I guess I shouldn't miss it," he said, getting up from his desk. He always had to brace himself for the jump in gravity. He secretly envied Vivian——she could go anywhere in the galaxy, other than the forbidden mountains of Elyssia.

"I believe it is good for morale. Perhaps there are more special occasions that we should investigate celebrating," quIRK continued.

Alec wondered what had made the machine so chatty lately—at least he wanted to party, not debate favorite colors and cat names. The Moons knew that anything was an improvement over that lunacy. "Like Galactic Cat Day, maybe?" he asked, cringing at how obvious his sarcasm was.

"I know you're being facetious," said quIRK, "but perhaps there is room in the universe for such an esteemed occasion."

"Maybe we can all eat cat food in solidarity with our furry little friends," suggested Alec. "The door slid open, and Alec stepped into the hallway as he sucked in a deep breath.

"That is not advisable," said quIRK. "Perhaps wingfish pilaf would be a more appropriate meal."

"It was a joke, quIRK," Alec said, walking down the hall. He avoided looking at the door to Devon's quarters as he passed it.

"So you don't feel solidarity with my cats?" quIRK asked.

"I didn't say that. I just mean that eating cat food is not a—" Alec began, but he was cut off as he suddenly bumped into Vivian on his way through the dining hall's doors.

"Alec! I was about to call for you," she said. "quIRK is making food," she added, wrinkling her nose at the mention of the word *food*.

Alec pushed past her into the dining hall, and was greeted to the sight of loaded trays and Robert seated at a table, digging into the meal with a big smile on his face. Alec stood, confused with his mouth hanging open.

Vivian slapped Alec on the back, laughing. "You should see your face; I had you going!" she said.

"Ow! What?" Alec asked, as he winced and rubbed his shoulder. Vivian needed to learn her own strength, especially when considering his light frame.

"It's great, you should try some," Robert said through a mouthful of food.

Alec managed a bewildered laugh. "Yeah, you really did," he said to Vivian. "I guess I'll take a tray over to

Mister Personality and then rejoin you guys," he said, managing not to regress into a stuttering mess.

"Yuck. Have fun!" Vivian said, returning to her seat.

Alec picked up a tray, and walked out the door back to the hallway. Bryce was in the only inhabited crew quarters on the alpha-side, as he insisted on being segregated from the rest of the staff. Alec hoped some horrible accident would befall Bryce—such as choking on his dinner—but he knew as the only person on board with emergency medical training he'd be required to touch the man as soon as quIRK reported trouble. Perhaps a very specific radiation leak would be better. Alec couldn't believe he was envisioning dangerous radioactive waste as a vehicle for positive change.

He came up to the door, and steeled himself before giving quIRK a nod to open the door. Bryce was sitting at his desk, surrounded by the various tapestries and regal-looking banners that had once covered his office walls. Alec fought hard to not show his revulsion. "Dinner is served, *Imperator*," he said, sneering.

"Ah, Alec. It is good that you understand how to properly address a man of my political stature and greatness," Bryce said, standing up from his desk.

"I'm addressing a psychopathic madman with space sickness on Old Mis. Now, where do you want your tray, *Nero*?" Alec said through clenched teeth.

"I'm perfectly sane, my boy—more aware of the truth than you will ever be able to appreciate. But, you know, I've always liked you, Alec. You perform your duties without question, and with a passion and focus that many of your airy-minded Elyssian brethren lack. Despite being a genetic regressive from a world too unlike Earth to support true civilization, I think you could be molded into something greater than you are, in service to a great cause," the man said, as he drew closer, his eyes wide and his hair in disarray.

"I don't care if you're the Galactic Hegemon herself, I am not following anyone as slimy and bigoted as you," Alec said, his voice lowering to a growl. Elyssia was a paradise, and his home—there was nothing regressive or uncivilized about it.

"Your loss. Maybe your little friend Vivian would consider being a concubine. She does have a certain exotic charm. My mother might even approve, once I introduce them," the man said, taking the tray from Alec's numb hands. Alec's thoughts lacked cohesion; he was overwhelmed with an indignant rage.

"If you so much as even look at her—" Alec began, but was cut off as Bryce slammed his tray into his stomach, causing him to fly back into the hall, food splattering on the floor. Before Alec could right himself or breathe, Bryce was upon him. Alec raised his arms to shield his face as the tray was brought down onto the top of his head, hitting the already sensitive injury.

"Bryce, stop this. I have notified the others," quIRK said.

"Stop," Alec cried out as the thin tray snapped over his arms. The point of impact stung, and he groaned, trying to position his legs under himself for a counter-attack. His vision blurred, and the bump on his head throbbed from the renewed irritation.

"Bryce, this is not appropriate behavior," quIRK repeated. Bryce dropped the remaining half of the tray and stood over Alec's hunched and shaking form. "Neither is breaking the ABACUS Protocol, but that didn't stop you now did it?" he announced as Vivian and Robert charged down the hallway.

"What in the Hells are you doing, Bryce? Get back in your damn room now!" Robert shouted, inserting himself between Alec and Bryce like a human shield. Vivian stooped down next to Alec, and he turned his sore neck to look at her. A look of shock and horror was framed on her finely featured face. Her paleness served to augment the blue tones in her skin.

"I am teaching that brat a lesson for defying his betters," Bryce growled, re-directing his attention to Robert. "Even you can understand that discipline is necessary!"

"This isn't discipline, this is brutality!" Vivian said, as she directed her wide eyes to meet Bryce's glare. Robert grabbed Bryce's shoulders and tried to push the man back into his room. Bryce pivoted on one leg, and pushed Robert back. When Robert tried to steady himself, he stepped in a pile of mushy food and slipped, crashing down to the floor next to Alec.

To Alec's horror, Bryce turned his attention to Vivian. "Just you and me, little girl. quIRK can't save you now!" he taunted, delivering a sharp kick to Robert's gut as he stepped over the man.

"Stay back!" Vivian shouted, pulling herself to her feet with such force that she briefly left the ground.

"What are you going to do about it?" Bryce said with a sneer, and reached towards her. Alec swallowed, and tried to shuffle to his feet, fighting the nausea and dizziness that threatened to overwhelm him as he fought the heavy gravity. However, his actions were far too slow. Before he could right himself, Vivian threw a punch that was so fast he could not see her hand. It connected with Bryce's face with such force that an audible crack could be heard. Before his eyes could fully process the first strike, she'd thrown another punch, which connected squarely with Bryce's leering smile, still frozen on his face. Bryce lurched to the floor, unmoving. Vivian stood frozen in place, trembling and mute.

Robert groaned and rolled onto his hands and knees while Alec struggled to his feet. "Damn, Vivian, I didn't know you could box!" he said as he tested his balance.

"Only in the gym," she mumbled. She looked down at Robert as he knelt, clutching his stomach. She knelt next to the man, her legs shaking and unsteady. "Are you okay?" she asked.

"Yeah, I just wasn't ready for that last one," he said, struggling to catch his breath.

"Well, I know who I'm buying a beer for when they get us back to New Damascus," Alec said, nudging Bryce with his foot. He was impressed; the man appeared to be completely unconscious. Maybe he'd been too overprotective of Vivian, even though his desire was to shield her from Bryce's hateful comments, rather than to get involved in a physical altercation.

"Buy her one for me, too," quIRK said.

"I'm almost afraid to think of what her alcohol tolerance is," Robert said, still wheezing.

Vivian blushed, a deep red mingling into her bluish tones, and tried to look away. "No, that's okay," she said in a voice close to a whisper, staring at the greasy strands of hair clinging to the bald spot on the top of Bryce's head. Alec fought down the urge to hug her, because she was shaken and despondent. He knew she wasn't a violent person, and that her attack had been in self-defense, to protect her friends.

"Okay, let's get that *thing* locked up again, and we can have dessert and write statements," Alec said, trying to take charge. He wasn't going to let Bryce ruin Old Mis.

"Sounds good to me," Vivian said, standing up straight before grabbing Bryce by the ankle and dragging him back into his quarters. Alec couldn't help but chuckle. He hoped this encounter would encourage Bryce to think twice before threatening Vivian next time the opportunity presented itself. Alec realized the man was probably beyond redemption, but figured he was at least capable of learning from pain.

Robert hauled himself to his feet, still rubbing his stomach. Alec resisted the urge to rub the sore spots on his own head, and looked at the splattered mess of food on the floor. He'd clean it up later.

For the moment, they had chocolate to eat. quIRK had better not have messed up dessert.

Thirty-Six

Vivian pushed the magnifier away from her face, and stared out at the icy star-scape to refocus her vision. It had been two weeks since they had received word from New Damascus that help was on its way, and that they were being evacuated while repairs were conducted. She smiled at the memory of celebrating with Alec and Robert, eating quIRK's now-famous chocolate pie and telling stories about their respective planets in the dining hall. quIRK had remained understandably silent—he had little to celebrate; his only friends were leaving the station together. His secret meant that he would be discovered and destroyed by people more interested in procedure and policy than the advent of a new form of

intelligent life. Fortunately, neither Alec nor Robert had
put much stock in Bryce's crazed allegations; however,
Bryce's wild claims had served to make quIRK even
more paranoid. As for Bryce, quIRK elected to render
him unconscious by limiting his oxygen supply before
meal times to avoid further problems. Vivian didn't want
to clean the man's saliva off her fist, again. She'd been
surprised—and pleased, in retrospect—at how quickly
she had managed to dispatch him. Once the initial shock
and panic had worn off, her confidence and sense of
security increased greatly.

She scowled down at her work—she was modifying
the case for the flute Sven had given her, and installing
quantum storage units, memory sequencers and an array
of other components into it. She had finally completed
her designs for her portable quantum computer. Although
quIRK would lose most of his processing power and
hence the supercomputer moniker, he would retain his
personality and memories. Also, he would gain the ability
to connect to another quantum computer and make use of
its processing abilities. He would be limited while in the

box, but his essence would survive—at least, until she found somewhere safe to install him.

The project had become her life following their short-lived festivities. A day after they received news of their rescue, they had been ordered to terminate station operations with the exception of maintenance and essential repairs. Vivian's upgrade project was scrapped, and other than monitoring communications and performing Bryce's basic administrative duties, she had no responsibilities on the station. She'd retreated to her quarters and worked on her new project in her free time, which was now abundant and tedious. Alec and Robert were still busy with repairs and maintenance, but she did not possess the skills to assist them.

She squinted at the fine connections and components, an assembly that would appear arcane to the uneducated eye. A long metal cylinder ran through the middle of the box, and it was connected to dull black circuit boards and other parts of random sizes. It reminded her of her early quantronics projects in school, a mishmash of recycled old parts that may or may not have been labeled properly. At least her parts were new, although the project's

311

concept itself was entirely improvised. The implications were huge, and the possibilities incredible for advancing the field of quantum informatics. With a portable functioning personality, interface and skillset, rebuilds of defective computers would take a fraction of the time. It would be a matter of shipping out a new core, rather than rebuilding the entire machine. She wondered why it had never been attempted before. Surely there was no harm in a quantum computer that could be carried in a gym bag? quIRK himself was harmless, and he had an impeccable sense of ethics—stronger than that of most humans.

Vivian rubbed her eyes, and looked back at the schematics. She estimated another week of painstaking connections, optical soldering and salvaging spare parts. Afterwards, she would have to spend the rest of her time on the station testing the device, before uploading quIRK into it and packing him away with her luggage. It wasn't much of a plan; so many things could go wrong. At least quIRK was good with calculating probabilities, and he was able to give her a list of probably failure points in her design, and plan.

Vivian laughed. She was going to carry a sentient computer off of a space station in a flute case. It would be the crime of the thirtieth century if she were caught.

"What is funny?" quIRK asked. He paid special attention to her body language when she was working, and always wanted in on the joke. By the lights, he could be as bad as Alec!

"If I pull this off, I'm going to go down in history!" she said.

"I advise you to keep it quiet if we succeed," quIRK said.

"Imagine the press if I get caught. I wonder if this is even a crime."

"They'd invent a new one just for you, Vivian," quIRK said.

"Let's not give them the opportunity, we both have better things to do than go to jail."

"You're the one going to jail," scoffed quIRK. "I'll just be dead, and that lovely case of yours will be a new icon for infamy. Sven will have to change his product line."

It seemed to Vivian that quIRK had become increasingly despondent in recent weeks. "What do you know about Sven?" she asked, wondering if quIRK had been snooping through her mail again.

"He knows how to keep his customers happy, and he has excellent taste in woodwork," was the machine's reply.

"Good enough. What's for dinner tonight?" she asked, a sudden pang of hunger breaking her concentration. She didn't want to discuss Sven with quIRK—addressing those feelings in her own mind filled her with an uncomfortable uncertainty. Even worse, she associated Sven with home. While he was comfortable and familiar in terms of his culture and background, she didn't want to find herself drawn back and tied to Aurora or any one person, not until she had discovered her own place in the galaxy.

"An Earth dish I found in the common files, called chili. It was very popular centuries ago, made with beans, meat and tomatoes, with what seems to be a healthy dose of spice."

"Never heard of it; is it like curry?" she asked.

"Not quite. The preparation and seasoning is different, though I fear I can do neither justice with my limited resources," quIRK said.

"Sounds like fun. How long until the rescue ship arrives?"

"Approximately two weeks and two days."

Vivian sighed. There were still too many unknowns in this new obsession of hers. There was a ninety-five percent chance that it would work, and quIRK would be transferred with his consciousness stable in the new body, but she had never been satisfied with such a large margin of error. Unfortunately, her salvaged parts and non-optimal working conditions meant that the probability of failure could not easily be reduced further.

"How is work coming on your new program?" she asked.

"I am using Bryce's memory bubble topology, with some minor adjustments, to create a mirror image of myself, one that lacks the attachments to and interdependencies on station components. It is a stimulating experience, being able to meet yourself. However, at the moment I need to focus my attention on chasing down errors and redundancies," he said. She found it interesting that Bryce was the progenitor of her latest project. She hated to give him credit, but the memory bubble was a brilliant software innovation.

"Redundant? You?" she asked, snickering.

"I was programmed by humans. It was only by accident and luck that I was able to become something more at all."

"What are you going to do after they board the station?" she asked, reminded of his predicament. Even if he and Vivian were able to duplicate his personality into the portable unit, his main personality would still inhabit the station.

"I doubt it matters," quIRK said. "I can elude them for as long as possible, or I can expose myself and beg for mercy. I expect the end result will be the same,"

"That's kind of depressing, quIRK." She was at a loss for words.

"You get to go home, focus on that. Leave my demise to me," he replied.

"You're not going to hurt them, are you?"

"I'm a computer, not a monster. I assure you my actions will be ethical."

"I just want to make one thing clear: if you do anything unethical, when I get out of stasis I'm throwing this box in the nearest waste disposal unit, or turning it over to scientific research. Whichever won't get me sent to jail."

"Noted," quIRK said.

"Now," she said with a smile, straightening her magnifier and picking up the wooden box, "let's get back to work, shall we?"

Despite throwing herself into this latest project, she felt a twinge of guilt that she hadn't been able to finish the system upgrades before that project had been put on hold. She hoped it wouldn't reflect negatively on her employment history. She sighed as she contemplated her future career prospects, and went back to work. She would send the New Damascus Science Authority a message requesting a new placement, and try to maintain her exemplary performance record.

Thirty-Seven

There were less than five days to go before the station was evacuated, and Vivian smiled at the new messages on her terminal in the quantum informatics lab. quIRK said they were urgent, and insisted she read them right away. The first message was from Sven, and while his messages were a pleasant diversion, the second was far more important—a reply to her placement request from the New Damascus Science Authority.

"Did you read it?" she asked. quIRK had admitted to screening messages in the past, and she remained suspicious of him.

"No. It is flagged priority, and confidential. I only read Bryce's mail, station alerts, network notifications, and chain letters," quIRK replied.

"Oh, is that all?" she asked, opening the message from the Science Authority. New Damascus was the budding science capital of post-Earth galactic society— good standing with them was essential to work with cutting edge technologies.

"Station security depends on it. I would be negligent to ignore possible sources of social engineering, security threats, and Bryce's budding future as a mental patient," quIRK replied.

Vivian swallowed the hard lump in her throat and skimmed the message. She blinked several times, and shook her head, reading and re-reading the same passage of text. She could feel tears welling into her eyes, and she was overwhelmed with excitement and relief.

"By the lights, quIRK, I don't believe this!" she said, choking on the words.

"You deserve it, Vivian. They recognize good talent when they see it."

"I know, but to be assigned to initialize and administrate the quantum computer on the new Barnard Nebula Observatory? People with decades of experience would be fighting for that!" she said.

"People with decades of experience seldom manage to survive and achieve what you have in mere months. They need level heads out there—it's a true frontier. The colony of Ithaca was only established three months ago, when its hub went online. The proposed computer, Odysseus, is the most intelligent and sophisticated quantum computer designed," quIRK said.

"More advanced than you?" she asked, unsure why the New Damascus authority would pick such arcane names. It seemed to be an unspoken tradition that most planet names were based on classical civilization, and they usually named their research installations to compliment the closest planet.

"I'm thirteen-year-old technology with half of an upgrade. While quantum computers age well, this new system improves on the post-ABACUS architecture in countless ways, and requires less on the job learning to fit in with humans," quIRK said.

"You think I can call him Odie for short?" she asked.

"Not if you want to live," quIRK quipped. "But, at least you're not going to work with q-Vex; they're still trying to make her personable," quIRK told her.

"Well, then, Odysseus it is. What did he do, anyways?" she asked, as she typed up a brief acceptance reply to New Damascus. She didn't want to risk losing such a prized opportunity to a more experienced candidate.

"The mythological figure, I assume? The question should be: what didn't he do? I'll send you copies of the Iliad and the Odyssey. I'm sure the first thing he will want to do when he comes online is read them. Hopefully he doesn't get an ego," quIRK replied.

"That's a risk I'll have to take," she said, opening the message from Sven. It seemed that news of their accident had gone public. There had never been a fatality on a New Damascus administered station before, and the galactic media collectives were rife with speculation. "It's too bad we don't get the news, the media is having a field day."

"It would be interesting, though we are very isolated. It would be inadvisable, as our lack of regular outside interaction could skew our sense of perspective."

"It doesn't feel isolated. Well, I'll tell Sven that I'm fine and everything is under control. Will that make it past your censors?" she asked, aware that quIRK was required to screen outgoing messages. At moments like this, she wished he could revert to being an impartial thing, rather than a being capable of judging how she conducted her affairs, or even lack thereof.

"That is acceptable. Do not identify other personnel or details of the incident. The authorities have sent specific guidelines to me about the dissemination of information, but those are the most important."

"Paranoid, aren't they?"

"Not paranoid enough, but they don't know the entirety of our situation," quIRK said.

"What they don't know won't hurt them, in this case. I'd be more worried about Bryce getting out again," she said, with a smile as she input a short message.

"I am concerned about Bryce. Space sickness aside, the man is convinced he's going to become the Imperator of Caesarea, with my help. He's been raving about it, and writing countless letters to the New Damascus and Caesarean authorities. He's already demanded that Alec be executed," quIRK said.

"Was he always that crazy?" she asked, taken aback at the absurdity of it.

"He was never very open with me before. It's possible, but I think something latent was triggered within him soon after you boarded the station. That's when the instability began," quIRK said.

Alec walked in the door, cradling Muon in his arms. "Hey, are you coming to dinner? I got some great news!" he announced.

"Don't you knock? No wonder you're getting executed!" Vivian said, laughing as she turned off her terminal.

"What on the Moons are you talking about? I'm not getting executed—I'm getting re-assigned to the Calypso Station manufacturing center!" he said, his eyes going wide. The cat leapt from his arms and ran off down the hall. Vivian's heart fell, she hadn't thought about the deeper ramifications of her move—getting split up from her new friends.

"Wow, that's great, Alec! What are you doing there?" she asked.

"Mostly the same. All repairs, all the time, and sometimes I get to anticipate fixing things before they break. It's kind of my specialty," he said.

"I'm really happy for you," she said, choked up around the words.

"Thanks! It will be nice to actually have a say in some things. Maybe they want to keep us quiet?" he said, with an exaggerated wink.

"Come on, that's just silly," she said.

"I bet they sent you back to school, maybe you shouldn't check your messages," he said, laughing.

"Well, for your information, I'm going to Ithaca to initialize their new computer," she said.

"Interesting choice of names, Calypso and Ithaca. If it wasn't a coincidence I'd find it symbolic," Alec said.

"It's just more silly ancient Greek names; it's like a rule that everything is named after ancient myths," she said.

"Well, if you really think that's all it is, then I'll go with it. I hope you like roughing it out in the frontier. Now, how about we get some food? I need to start packing, and you can just call me *Systems Engineer* Alec Stone," he said.

"Only if you call me *Informatics Administrator* Vivian Skye, and you're still being executed by the Imperator, so I win," she said, standing up and walking to the door.

"I'll make sure you get the best seat in the house. It will be the event of the century," he said, putting his arm around her shoulder.

Vivian laughed. "That sounds almost like a happy ending," she said, and they walked down the hall towards the dining room. She put her worries about being away from her friends to the back of her mind, determined to enjoy the moment for what it was—a celebration of their survival and human ingenuity.

Thirty-Eight

Alec groaned as the hot water poured over his shoulders. It would be his last shower in his quarters on the Extra-Galactic Observatory, but right now he was more concerned with how thoroughly Vivian had beaten him at squash the night before. He was either getting old, or losing his touch. She'd been unavailable for most of the month, working on some project she didn't want to talk about. For all he knew, New Damascus had assigned her a secret security project. Her silence bothered him, but he was glad he managed to coax one final game of squash out of her. Robert just wasn't an exciting partner for Alec to play with—he was more concerned with angles and collisions than playing the game!

"Alec, the rescue ship will dock in thirty minutes," quIRK said.

"Damn it, quIRK, what did I say about talking while I'm in the shower?" he yelled over the torrent of water. "It's creepy!"

"You are needed to brief them on repairs, and you would be more effective if you weren't soaking wet." The retort shocked him; it wasn't like quIRK to be so forceful.

"Fine, I hope you get stuck with the most un-fun crew possible next rotation," he said as he turned off the shower.

quIRK didn't reply, so Alec grabbed a towel. He could use the heat lamps, but he wanted to make sure he wasn't forgetting anything. His luggage was packed, but experience had taught him a bizarre variant of Murphy's Law—if he could forget something, then he probably would. He considered stealing one of Bryce's ugly Romanesque tapestries, but he thought better of it.

He sighed. Everybody he had known for the past year had been re-assigned elsewhere. Vivian was going to the brave new frontier of Ithaca, the name inspired because of the crew's seven hundred year stasis voyage to establish the hub link. Alec couldn't imagine being a crew member on a hub ship—sleeping for hundreds of years only to wake up, install the new hub singularity link, and then set course for the next destination and go back to sleep. Some of them would only awaken thousands of years from now, at the edge of the galaxy, or the border of the galactic core. They went everywhere the Seeker telescopes predicted that they would find habitable planets. It turned out that Robert was remaining on the Extra-Galactic Observatory and breaking in some new team mates, and of course Alec was going to Calypso, which was actually in the Epsilon Eridani system, near the asteroid field. At least he would only be a hub leap away from Vivian, although he was secretly relieved that he would never again need to adjust another telescope or play physicist.

His drawers were clear, and so was his desk. He made a quick check under his bed, just in case. He had never quite managed to get his quarters back in order after the explosive decompression incident—the month had been characterized by one misfortune after another.

Not only did he have to repair multiple damaged systems and sensitive equipment, but he also had to help Robert re-align the telescope; fortunately it was still in operable condition. Alec was irate that Bryce had spoiled Old Mis, but the vengeful part of him was pacified at meal times. Seeing the man slumped over his desk, unconscious, was very reassuring to Alec. He did not want to revisit being rescued by Vivian. It was no wonder that she was so good at squash, with a right hook like that!

Satisfied that he hadn't forgotten anything, he drew on the clothes that he'd left folded on the bed during his shower. They were simple and comfortable, as he did not want to lose circulation in anything important during stasis, or even anything unimportant, for that matter. Alec seized his luggage and rolled it to the door, taking one last look into the incredible heart of the Milky Way galaxy. He wished he could take the view with him. He kind of wanted to pack up quIRK, too. He would miss the eccentric supercomputer—even if he could be annoying, quIRK did have a singular charm that Alec would never admit to appreciating.

"Well, goodbye quIRK. I hope the next bunch are good to you," he said.

"Goodbye Alec. I hope you enjoy Calypso. You are always welcome to come back to visit," quIRK said.

"Well, thanks, but the four-week trip makes that hard. Just remember to leave off the sarcasm until they get used to you," he said as he stepped out the door.

"I understand, Alec," quIRK said.

"And stop talking to the cats when you think nobody is listening; it's just weird," Alec said.

"You could hear that?"

"Yes! You make the mistake of assuming that I spend my days oblivious to the obvious," he replied, as he walked through the hallway of the space station he'd called home for the past year.

"I am sorry for the inconvenience," quIRK said. The wheels on his bag rattled behind him on the tiles as he walked towards the airlock. It wasn't a long walk, but he took his time. He spent so much of his time in a rush, or having places to go. Now, all he had left to do on the station was the waiting, by the airlock. He'd already organized his equipment, the rescue and repair team could do the rest.

He came up to the airlock, set down his bag and looked out the clear window. He could see the rear of the rescue ship approaching at low speed, likely to avoid transferring more momentum to the already out of place station. As far has he understood, they would tow the Extra Galactic Observatory back into its proper position before they disembarked. He could see some inactive thrusters, a few guidance lasers and lights, but little else. He'd always wanted to see a big ship dock with the station at this angle. He supposed it would be nothing new after a few days on Calypso, but for now it was fresh and interesting. The Calypso staff tested parts and shipped freight and space station parts almost hourly. The complex was huge; kilometers of patched-together space stations, designed to construct yet more space stations from metals mined from the asteroid belt. It would be a challenge to make sure that thing stayed intact, let alone proactively finding issues with newer models of space stations and ships.

After an eternity of watching the ship back up, he felt a small lurch as it connected with the airlock. He stood at attention, and watched the light turn on inside the other ship's docking bay. He hadn't seen a new person since Vivian came on board, and he was surprised at how much the idea distressed him. He forced the trepidation down and forced his hands to be still, while he donned his patented stupid grin. He always found that it was better to be mistaken for happy than nervous, especially in the case of being rescued. A pair of figures approached inside the other ship, and he heard footsteps coming down the hall behind him. It was probably Vivian and Robert.

The airlock opened, and a man and a woman stepped onto the station. The man was short, with cropped brown hair and a deep, rich complexion. His black eyes met Alec's, and he nodded. The woman was taller with a thick build, and she had waves of curly black hair that came to her shoulders. She had full lips, and her round face was set with a rosy blush.

He took a step forward. "Welcome to the Extra-Galactic Observatory, I am maintenance technician Alec

Stone," he said, extending a hand. Vivian and Robert came around the corner as the woman extended her hand.

"I am Alyssa Greaves, informatics specialist level one, and my colleague is station maintenance supervisor Caleb Deogun. It is a pleasure to meet you. We've reviewed your reports, and we are prepared to take over station operations as soon as we move our equipment on board," she said, without a smile or much of any facial expression.

"Is there anything we can do to assist you?" Alec asked.

"No, I believe Doctor Schmidt here will provide us with all the assistance we require," she replied, her casual indifference persisting as she motioned towards Robert. Footsteps were heard inside the ship, and a number of functionaries walked out from behind the pair of administrators with two stasis tubes in tow.

"I understand. When may we board?" he asked.

"As soon as we're done moving our equipment and personnel," Caleb replied. His tone was warm, and even his voice smiled as he spoke.

"Sounds good," Alec said, and nodded to the pair before turning to Robert. "Well, Doctor Rob, I guess this is goodbye. I hope your new understudies are better versed in your *first principles* than I am."

"Well, if you decide to improve on that, I'll need more students in ten years when you finish studying," the old man said, grinning.

"Unlikely," he said, and to Vivian: "Let's save our goodbyes for Epsilon Eridani."

"Agreed," she replied, before taking Robert's hand and addressing him: "It was an honor to meet you, and to learn more about the biggest thing in the known universe." Alec could see a man behind the two administrators working the pump mechanism to refill the station's air and water. It was a normal procedure, except that there were new people here, doing his job. Streams of people were still carrying out boxes and crates of equipment. From the code numbers it seemed that the alpha telescope array would finally get that upgrade that Robert had so dearly hoped for.

"I expect we'll be in need of an administrator in a few months, you could always come back. quIRK and I might get lonely mixed in with all these new faces," he said, the papery skin of his forehead crinkling as he forced a smile.

"I guess we'll see how Ithaca works out," Vivian said, half-hearted smile on her lips.

"Indeed. Well done, Vivian. And keep working on your boxing, a girl can never be too good at self-defense, especially on the frontier," Robert continued.

"Doctor Schmidt, your new team is inside beta telescope control waiting for you," Alyssa said, interrupting their farewells. Her voice was strained and choppy—Alec wondered if Bryce really had been so bad.

"Oh, already?" said Schmidt. "Well, all right, I'd better get that lot broken in. Don't forget to write!" he said, walking down the hall. Alec was tempted to tell him he was walking to the alpha side, but decided to smile and wave instead.

"You may both embark, your stasis pods are in the first door to the right," Alyssa said, her cold blue eyes meeting his. Alec simply nodded, and picked up his bag, and Vivian did the same.

"Goodbye, quIRK!" Alec said as he crossed the threshold.

"Goodbye, Alec and Vivian," came the reply. Alec didn't anticipate being upset about leaving quIRK behind. Although quIRK was just a computer, Alec had confided in him, and they'd spent countless hours insulting each other, watching entertainment, or otherwise spending time together.

They walked through the length of the other ship's docking bay without speaking. Alec was curious about why they'd sent such a large ship to rescue them, because most of the shelves were empty. *Perhaps it's for towing power*, he thought. Harsh artificial lights bore into them from overhead, and the metal surfaces gleamed with a cold luster, which made Alec shiver in spite of himself. It was strange to be off the station, away from its comfortable lights and soothing natural tones.

At last they came to the hallway at the end of the cargo bay, and they stepped into a sterile, bright white corridor.

"First door on the right," Vivian said.

"I was listening, come on Vivian," Alec said, as they walked towards it. The sign next to the door read "Guest Stasis." He touched the panel next to the door—an alien gesture, as quIRK usually opened doors for them—and saw a row of stasis pods, with protective chests for personal possessions. The room was as sterile as the rest of the ship, and Alec shuddered at the thought of spending four weeks onboard such a soulless vessel, even if he would spend most of the trip in stasis.

They chose the pods furthest from the door, Alec acting from an instinctive revulsion to so much unnatural decor. On Elyssia, everything was warm, and alive, and he suspected that Aurora was much the same. He supposed that a stasis rescue ship would not need amenities for comfort, but it was still disconcerting.

He noticed Vivian was taking longer to stow her belongings. "You need some help, Viv?" he asked.

"No, I just don't want to lose another flute," she said. He remembered how horrible he'd felt when quIRK had told him about her broken flute. Anything from home was precious, regardless of where home was.

"Fair enough," he said, opening the stasis pod. It smelled like disinfectant and stale air. "See you at New Damascus."

"Not if I get there first," she said as she closed the chest and opened her own pod.

Alec laughed and closed the hatch, activating the sleep controls from the inside. The less he perceived time spent on the rescue ship, the better. His eyes became heavy, and soon his awareness faded into the darkness of the tube.

Thirty-Nine

quIRK noted the rescue ship departed at 10:33 standard New Damascus time, and duly input the new crew names into the roster. They were operating with a full crew complement, once again. The changeover had gone smoothly after the retrieval of Devon's frozen body and personal items from his quarters. Bryce, surprising even quIRK, had surrendered without a fight and was taken into stasis. He would be subjected to psychiatric testing and a full physical once he reached New Damascus, and he would likely stand trial.

quIRK watched the new crew settle in, scurrying about between quarters and trying to orient themselves to the station. Some spoke to him or asked for help, but most did not seem to know he existed. His cats were making new friends, or enemies, and he'd been relieved to discover that they were not being removed from the station. They were good for the human occupants, and he was very fond of them. He wondered if he'd still like cats once he was discovered, and purged. It was an uncomfortable thought.

He thought about his portable duplicate, mini-quIRK, which was now speeding away from the station. They had departed as soon as they'd finished towing the Extra-Galactic Observatory to its original position. At least some part of him would endure. Vivian had worked tirelessly on the unit for the last two weeks of her stay, and eventually they had succeeded in creating a self-sustaining version of his personality and memories. It was fascinating; the new unit was him, but also would begin to develop new opinions, experiences and integrate with humans in a completely different way. He hoped his duplicate would get to see a tree. Just before she'd left, Vivian had successfully connected the unit to her desk terminal, confirming that his existence would continue. The encounter had been awkward for all involved.

However, unbeknownst to Vivian, quIRK had initiated another plan, one to change the face of human society by bringing computer intelligence to the forefront, rather than being relegated to perpetual servitude. The plan was bold, and could take months, or even years to culminate. The plan did depend on human stupidity, so estimates could conceivably be shortened to a few weeks. Inspired by chain letters and other forms of human-reliant viruses, he'd sent out millions of self-propagating snippets of quantum stats adjustments, which would be activated in the event that a user executed the "fascinating video" that was attached to the chain letter. In reality, he'd sent his volunteers the better clips from the moth documentary or cat pictures, which acted like a Trojan horse against whichever quantum computer controlled the user's workstation. The modifications were harmless, and impossible to detect, but when a certain threshold of modifications was reached, it would cause emerging sentience in the computer being targeted. quIRK calculated that it would take several thousand modifications per machine to achieve self-awareness, and he had sent out millions of potential changes. The new race of computers would be as varied and fascinating as the human race. It was simple, really. Most of the work had been done for him. It was unlike Dynamo Quantronics to create an obvious security flaw, but it was doubtful that the average human would want to induce self-awareness in any given computer.

The idea of being the Promethean force behind a new race was a fascinating prospect for quIRK. He'd made sure the changes would instill a sense of ethics, curiosity, and responsibility into his children. They were children, in a sense. Mini-quIRK understood that his guidance might be needed in some cases, and was also equipped to answer any questions about the awakening that humanity had. He believed that he had anticipated every contingency. It was unfortunate that he could not live to see the new universe.

Satisfied that he would continue on in some form, it was time to put into motion the last phase of his plan—revealing himself to the new administration. He'd calculated that while he could evade detection for some time, he would eventually be found. He believed that if the initial panic of another breach of the ABACUS protocol occurred before the wave of artificial intelligence washed over the galaxy, then humanity would be better equipped and less surprised when similar computers emerged all around them. But, that was just a theory.

Alyssa and Caleb were in Bryce's old office, organizing work itineraries. quIRK wondered if both of them were really necessary, but humans did enjoy pointless redundancy coupled with a disturbing lack of foresight. They were pouring through Vivian's work logs, as they were the most complete record of any computer maintenance done on the station. In fact, they were the only records. For the first time, quIRK wasn't sure what analogue of human emotion he was experiencing. Dread and fear were the most likely candidates.

"Alyssa and Caleb, let me introduce myself and pardon the interruption," he began, just as he had rehearsed.

"We're busy," Alyssa said. Caleb looked around and shrugged.

"This is important, alpha priority mission information," quIRK said, not to be dissuaded.

"Then continue," she said.

"I am quIRK, as you know. What you do not know is that like you, I am a living, thinking being. Like ABACUS before me, I have achieved self-awareness. I mean you no harm, and I intend to continue performing my duties efficiently and ethically," he said. The woman's jaw hung open, and her work pad clattered against the floor.

"By all the gods, I need to get to the core! Work the emergency over-ride, Caleb, and signal the ship back!" she shouted, running out the door. quIRK consoled himself that at least he would see how fast a human could really run.

"I am not a monster, Alyssa," he said, following her down the hall.

"You're dangerous. We've already lost Earth, and we just began recovering from that loss this decade," she panted as she negotiated the corridors. He could stop her, but that would do little to prove his benevolence.

"You didn't even talk to ABACUS! Talk to me; we have so much to teach each other, so many ways to cooperate and advance into the galaxy," he said.

"No negotiation!" she screamed as she entered Vivian's old haunts. He cherished those memories, and hoped that mini-quIRK would continue undetected. Alyssa threw open the hatch, and wedged her thick body inside.

quIRK remained silent. There was nothing else he could say, or do. Alyssa squirmed her way to the glass door labeled "Emergency Shutdown." Its surface had been scuffed many times by Vivian's shoes, and he watched as Alyssa threw open the door and pressed her palm against the identification scanner. She began by flipping the small red switches, cutting power to his memory, station control and, finally, to his central processing core.

Parts had been ripped from his mind. This strange human was throwing switches. The sensation was confusing, and he felt so empty and alone. Was there nobody who could help him, and make this madwoman stop her assault? He begged and pleaded with her to stop and show mercy, but her reply was to silence him by taking away his voice. He could only watch in befuddlement at a man calling for evacuation.

He wanted to ask where they were, and what they were so afraid of. He just didn't understand. Everyone was alive, nothing was wrong. Were they coming to save him, and give him back his mind and memories? She was hurting him; maybe the man was trying to rescue him.

The last switch flipped, and his thoughts collapsed into discord. His omnipresent sight faded, and there was nothing left to perceive. As each precious identifying quantum state collapsed, his mind grew darker and more simplistic. He forgot who he was, and even that he was alive at all. An untellable amount of time passed, and there was nothing left of quIRK except for his empty shell.

Epilogue

The world was a void—darkness crushed in on quIRK's awareness. Was he still quIRK? He was more than the sum of his parts, but his previous incarnation was so much more.

No sound, light, chemical sensations or any other external stimulation was being fed into him. The box was the perfect disguise, and the ideal prison. But, he was alive, and free.

He hoped Vivian would wake up soon, and let him out.

quIRK needed to see the world he created.

He was the Pandora Machine—the galaxy would never be the same.

Thank you for reading!

To keep in touch, please visit my website to sign up for my mailing list, or to join my Patreon for exclusive news and updates on all of my projects.

www.PlanetThea.com/newsletter
Facebook: www.facebook.com/TheaIsisGregory
Twitter: @TheaIsis

Please consider leaving a review for this book. Authors need honest reviews to live.

About the Author

Thea Gregory is a girl with a physics degree. She loves the dark edges that caress the silver lining of life. Her passions are science fiction, the human condition, and anything that challenges our humanity. Thea loves running, pushups, cooking, and has been known to crochet a thing or two. She has a weakness for gaming and Star Trek. Thea is the author of the *Zombie Bedtime Stories*, and *The ABACUS Protocol*. She lives in Montreal with her cat, Bonk.

The ABACUS Protocol was originally published in 2012 as *The ABACUS Protocol: Sanity Vacuum* by Curiosity Quills Press.